LIGGERS & DREAMERS

First Edition
Thin Man Press London 2015
© Josie Demuth
Josie Demuth is hereby identified as author of these works
in accordance with the Copyright, Designs and Patents Acts, 1988.
The author has asserted her moral rights.
No part of this publication may be reproduced, stored in a retrieval
system, or transmitted, in any form or by any means without the prior
written permission of the publisher.
A CIP catalogue record for this title is available from
the British Library

ISBN 978-0-9930141-4-7
Thin Man Press
London
www.thinmanpress.com

Liggers & Dreamers

By Josie Demuth

Any resemblance to real persons either living or dead is entirely coincidental

Cover illustration © Jason Gibilaro 2015

The e-mail

From: Nuisance Busters

Bcc: Gallery directors, Cork Street, London W1

Subject: Cork Street Liggers List

Recommended action: Look out for these jokers at Private Views, and inform them that their company is not required

1. The Golden Oldie: Meryl is the number one ligger. This assessment based on frequency of sightings of this individual at private events over the past six months, glasses of wine and champagne consumed, and number of regrettable incidents caused by her antics. Our hearts went out to the Huntington Gallery, who had the task of peeling this undignified seventy-something year old off the drinks table last week. She had passed out on her back, and her snores were off the Richter scale. Please don't feel sorry for her. She is nothing but a nuisance and will trash your event.

2. Two Birds, One Stone: Baddie and Eustacia. We had never been intoxicated by somebody's breath alone before we met Eustacia. It's like there's a brewery in her gut. Her boyfriend Baddie, is one of the ringleaders of the ligging scene. Don't let him bullshit you that what he's up to is some 'performance art'. A no-nonsense approach is required here.

3. Buffalo Bill (aka Richard Nolan-Wickes): Apologies for the quality of this pic. To clarify - Richard bears a remarkable resemblance to the tranny serial killer in *Silence Of The Lambs*. Rumour has it that he is actually a very wealthy man, with a pad over in Holland Park. Nevertheless, he is on the scrounge every night, and will stop at nothing to avoid denting his fortune.

4. The Young British Artist (YBA): This saddo likes to pretend he is still a big wig in the contemporary art world. The Dom Dicker gallery was hot for a nano-second back in the nineties. We're told that this was solely because Dom was desperately handing out cocaine to YBAs in an attempt to make them like him. Unfortunately for this ligger, nobody cares to remember his generosity.

5. Bonkers Bonnie: What a sweet name for such a monstrous individual. This one wants you to believe she is an architect. But relax, even your dizziest intern won't be fooled. This nut once tried to bottle one of our nuisance busters at an event a couple of years back. The reason? He ate the last prawn tempura. She still haunts our nightmares.

6. The Chinese Charlatan: Who wants to be a millionaire? Well, we all could be if we were to charge Tony Phun for the canapés, champagne and cocktails he has deceived his way into consuming over the years. This audacious Chinaman lists himself as a Director of a very famous Knightsbridge department store on his personal website. The only event he should be attending is his prosecution in court for fraudulent behaviour.

7. The Loser: This Indian, known to his ligger chums as Ashpak, is not, repeat not, an art collector. That's all we have to say on the matter.

8. Screamy: Simon Baldwin is hysterical, gobby and gay (as anything). Wino Simo often drives around in a Rolls with his Housemate (see Buffalo Bill). Don't be deceived. He is a parasite, wholly dependent on galleries (the ever-reluctant host) for survival.

9. The Extremist: Peter Corbitt will stop at nothing to get at what he craves. He is a fundamentalist ligger, on a constant pilgrimage to enter your event. Be thorough. Take your time. Ask questions. Do not, under any circumstances, let him palm himself off as a big cheese.

10. Loopy and Loopier: The Aussie, known as Mac, is canny. He will court door staff with tales from other events (that he has crashed) and before they know what's hit them, he'll be inside hoovering up canapés. He seems to have his sights set on bagging **failed artist** 'Grettil' as his girlfriend - this one's not only a ligger, but hostile and violent. They should both come with a warning label.

11. The Angry Dandy: His name is William and he wears tweed. Serial wino. Yet if you dare to politely request that he remove himself from your own event, you should have an umbrella handy for the inevitable downpour of saliva-coated abuse you will have to endure.

12. The Rectangular Regular: Stout and boxy, this one's not easy to overlook. If you miss Audrey elbowing her way towards the drinks table, you'll certainly hear her booming her critique of the art world 'elite' (while stealing their nibbles).

13. Irreverent George: Priest by day, thief by night. This fully paid up member of the Church of England clergy is a veteran deceiver of gallery staff with his dog collar and pious smile. Who me? A ligger? It is a most convincing get up and we can see why he regularly passes through your doors unchall-enged. Let me tell you now, the Reverend George will enter your event, savage the freebies, wipe his mouth on his cassock sleeve and leave without so much as a glance at your exhibition. Now you know where his true intentions lie, you can turn him away with a clear conscience.

14. The Sheep: A dedicated follower of the ligger leaders, Deborah is always in tow. This frizzy-haired pest can usually be found propped up against a pillar, or sometimes a valuable artwork, wasting an expensive glass of champagne.

Deborah

The night was still young and the liggers scurried through the back streets of Mayfair, the narrow pavements illuminated by well-lit designer boutiques' windows.

Upon reaching Piccadilly they waited for the thunder of red double-decker buses to roll past before they crossed the road, hopping onto the pavement just outside the Ritz and making their way down St James's Street.

Nearest the road, was Peter Corbitt, a short weedy man in his mid-fifties, with a head of wispy white hair. He walked with a sense of great urgency, his neck arched downwards below his pointed shoulders, while his beady eyes glinted ahead into the night. To his right strode the tall lanky frame of Mac Johnson the Australian; his suit trousers flapped above his ankles and his gold tie streamed out behind him.

Next to Mac, the rotund figure of Deborah scuttled along the shadowy side of the pavement, the street lights catching the edges of her red fluffy hair.

The three contrasting silhouettes were united by one common purpose.

"Now, just breeze through looking straight ahead," said Peter, unzipping his anorak and stuffing it into his rucksack, revealing his trusty nylon George suit jacket. "They shouldn't ask any questions. I just got a text from Alexia and she got straight in."

"Wow, good on her," said Mac, eyebrows raised on a handsome, but well-weathered face that had obviously taken a battering from the storms of London nightlife.

"Brrrrr," Deborah shivered, suddenly pinched by a frosty breeze. Then she remembered. "I left my coat in Timothy Taylor's. Shit!"

"We'll get it later," said Peter, smoothing out his jacket as he walked.

"It shuts at eight, that's in an hour," she protested.

"Well, we can't wait for you, it's all about timing," said Peter looking to Mac for support.

"This is *Charlie's*," asserted Mac in his strong Melbourne accent. "This is London's biggest Fine Art auction house we're talking about here - I mean, it's gonna be the best party in town Deborah."

"Oh forget it," said Deborah decisively; other concerns now displaced by new exciting prospects. "What shall we say if they ask us for names?"

"Ali Vivieri," said Mac, "he's got to be on the guest list."

"Yes he gets all the invites," Deborah concurred. "So what about a woman for me?"

"Agh God," moaned Mac. "What about that woman from Bill Brown Gallery. Ah damn, what's her name?"

"Elizabeth... Enfield?" Peter offered, combing his white hair to the side.

"Earnshaw," Mac corrected him. "Elizabeth Earnshaw, yeah good call. I spotted her in the Bill Brown Gallery earlier when we were walking past - it didn't look like they'd be wrapping up for quite a while. I'll be someone's plus one... I bet they're both allowed plus ones."

"Oh they will be, absolutely," said Peter knowledgably

They turned the corner at the foot of St James's where they could see a queue stemming from an illuminated canopied entrance. Black cabs and Mercedes pulled up at the venue depositing well-groomed individuals some of whom went to the back of the queue while others, possessed of a greater sense of entitlement, simply strode to the front and went straight in. The liggers were no strangers to crashing high profile events and walked down the line of be-suited men wearing bow ties and ladies in satin dresses and fur coats with an air of casual expertise. As they joined the end of the queue, Deborah smoothed her black woolen skirt, picking at the protruding bobbles.

"I'm relying on this for dinner," she warned the two men, clutching at her rumbling stomach. "They didn't have any canapés at Timothy Taylor's."

Peter nudged her and nodded in the direction of a tall man in front. Standing on her tiptoes she peaked over the collar of his overcoat, and was disconcerted to see that he held, in his leather-gloved hand, a large oblong golden invitation. The three exchanged looks.

"It'll be okay," said Mac reassuringly as they inched towards the glow of the open doors. "You've just gotta be assertive."

Peter, on the other hand, was not so relaxed about this development. He pulled out his wallet and began to rifle through his collection of tattered business cards.

"I wonder if there's a card I can use," he muttered. "I don't think Ali Viriani ever gave me one."

Deborah reached for her own wallet. "Not a bad idea," she muttered, eyebrows raised as she shuffled through her own deck, compiled over many years of drinking in West End galleries. But it was too late for deliberation, they had reached the front. The doormen, dressed in tail coats and red satin bowties, unclipped the velvet rope and the trio stepped through uncertainly. They ascended the grand staircase to the famous auction rooms, dazzled by the dancing light from two enormous sparkling chandeliers.

"Wow," breathed Mac. "I should have brought my shades, eh?"

As the three colluders approached the magnificent arched threshold, they slowly became aware of five tall stands in front of them, each manned by a member of staff leafing through folders of printed names. Deborah started to back away but Mac gripped her arm.

"Come on!" he whispered.

An immaculate oriental lady stepped forward. She wore an elegant midnight blue satin evening gown which looked as though it had melted over her slender frame. Her dark silky hair was twisted into a delicate swirl with a chopstick, not a strand out of place.

"Which guest list are you on gentlemen… and Madame?" her accent was French, her tone reserved.

Peter gaped at the petite host, until Mac poked him in the ribs. "This one," Peter spluttered, withdrawing a card from his pack and thrusting it in her face. She cleared her throat and took the card with her satin gloved hand. After what seemed like a lifetime, she handed back the card and beamed.

"Mr Schwartz!" she exclaimed. The staff all looked up from their folders, suddenly alert. They raised their eyebrows and grinned in unison.

"Yes," croaked Peter doubtfully.

"Allow me to introduce myself. I am Violette Wu. We have not had the pleasure of welcoming you at Charlie's before. But let me tell you, we have been patiently awaiting your good company for quite some time"

"I'm-very-busy," stammered Peter.

Violette Wu clasped his arm and shook her head in a feverish demonstration of understanding.

"Of course! Now, please just step right through. I take it these are your guests?"

A silence ensued. Peter began to nod frantically, a fixed grin across his pasty freckled face. Deborah stuck her hand up in a wave, giggling awkwardly.

"Hello," boomed Mac lunging forward to extend his wave into an overly firm handshake. Violette winced in pain and retrieved her hand before smoothing over the embarrassing moment with a warm and welcoming laugh. The three intruders joined in with a chorus of cackles.

"Thank you," Peter blurted eventually as they were led to the next grand mahogany staircase, carpeted in an elegant lilac shade. "Busy night, eh?" He managed with a strained chortle.

"I shall leave you here, Mr Schwartz," she smiled, touching his arm gently and leaning in closer. "And yes, but remember we are never too busy to better acquaint you with the artworks."

She nodded at Mac and Deborah before sailing back to the entrance.

"I think you're in there Peter!" exclaimed Mac as they ascended the staircase.

"What the hell did you give her?" hissed Deborah.

"I don't know, Marcus gave it to me the other night because I helped him get into a business convention in the Gherkin. He said it was my *'Get out of jail free card',*" replied Peter, giggling with elation.

"Or get into *Charlie's* free card," laughed Mac.

As they sailed through the bustling auction rooms, the mystery of the business card became a distant memory as the finest canapés swirled around them and champagne glasses glided under their noses and into their hands.

They discovered fellow liggers in other rooms where they congratulated each other on getting into the event. They exchanged tales of the many who had perished at the guest lists and those who had even tried the back doors.

"Apparently Richard actually pretended to be from the catering company," said their friend Meryl, a tall elderly lady and one of London's most robust gate-crashers.

"Yes, but then they asked him the name of the company and he didn't know!" said Alexia, a frizzy-haired painter. They all erupted into laughter and chinked their champagne glasses together, full of mirth, triumph and gratitude that they had not, themselves, been unmasked.

"To Charlie's!" they toasted.

"And to Schwartz," added Peter.

"What, Damien Schwartz?" said Alexia dryly.

"That is correct," said Peter, producing the card from his pocket.

"He actually gave *you* his card?"

"No, Marcus gave it to me the other night. Christ knows where he got the thing, it's probably been passed around everyone we know. Who the hell is he anyway?"

"I think he's some big art dealer," replied Alexia. "I'm sure he was on the 'Art Review Power 100' list."

They all shuffled closer to get a glimpse of the card.

DAMIEN SCHWARTZ
SCHWARTZ EDITIONS
damien@schwartzeditions.com
New York: +1 646 68 43 56 7
Beijing: +86 10 234 3458
Paris: +33 123 56789

"Can't you keep on pretending to be him and buy all my art?" asked Alexia dolefully. The group laughed and a waiter stopped to offer them a platter of seared tuna kebabs, only to find himself with an empty tray in a matter of seconds.

"Like a pack of seagulls," sneered a lady in a long, pale pink sequined dress as she passed with a friend, but every group member was in a state of such intense pleasure that they could not connect with the emotions required to care. Nothing felt better to them than crashing Charlie's and basking in the free champagne, canapés and highly sought-after art. This was, quite simply, an art ligger's Everest and they had conquered it.

Audrey

Some nights later, Audrey shook with laughter as she stood among a group of friends in the Albatross Gallery, Cork Street. Big drops of wine slopped freely over the rim of her glass, as she guffawed. It was one of those perfect nights in the West End, she reflected happily - something that was becoming increasingly rare of late. A good combination of friends had assembled in the centre of the space and the wine was superb.

"Shame about the art," said Audrey, her thoughts continuing out loud. She raised, above the rim of her glasses, a greying eyebrow which had not quite been disguised by the thin brown lines of a khol pencil hurriedly applied on the bus.

The group looked at their surroundings. Brash, cartoon-like images of London, Dubai and Sydney glared at them from the walls. Some of these horrors had even incorporated McDonald's signs into the landscape.

Audrey shuddered in her navy and tan coloured dress. The fitted garment accentuated her short, yet robust form and her long straight brown hair hung over the fabric in two symmetrical curtains.

"It's dreadful," agreed Moira, a flame-haired painter. "All the really good artists we know, and this is what floats to the top."

"Well it's certainly popular," said Audrey, gesticulating at the tiny red dots on the wall underneath nearly every piece. Wine sloshed in a semi-circle around them. "A load of banks probably bought them for their offices," grumbled Thomas, their bald Swiss companion. "It's all the same bowl of soup."

They tutted, and glugged from what remained in their glasses. A gallery assistant emerged from the kitchen with a tray of canapés and the group were quick to surround her.

Audrey quickly devoured the two pieces of toast and smoked salmon that she had retrieved and sighed as she caught sight of the now empty tray, yards ahead.

"Just a couple of crumbs," she moaned.

"It's every twenty minutes on the dot they bring out these out," Moira observed, disconsolately.

It was approaching eight o'clock and Audrey and Moira decided to reccy the space in search of a final top up. The two women were old friends, they had met at a private view back in the early nineties when Moira asked Audrey where she had bought her lime-coloured hipsters. The rest was history... most of which they could not remember.

"So how have you been sweetheart?" asked Moira.

"Oh struggling on. Trying to sue my boss," said Audrey. "Then hopefully I can make some art, and be a perfect grandma."

"And how is the baby?" asked Moira.

"Yep. Good. Wonderful. You know, I was born to be a grandma."

"Oh yes. Of course darlin'," said Moira, patting her arm and smiling fondly.

"I'm going to show him the way. Stop him from being one of the herd... ," said Audrey firmly.

"Well, perhaps you should introduce him to Thomas," said Moira picking up some papers from the reception desk and flicking through them absent-mindedly. Suddenly she froze.

"...I think my grandson's going to change the consciousness of the world, Moira. I can really feel it," Audrey enthused dreamily. "He doesn't want Peppa Pig, he wants Blake... ," she noticed her companion's horrified expression and took hold of her arm. "What? What's wrong?"

"Audrey, look at this!" squeaked Moira, clutching the papers with white knuckles.

"What is it? Oh, it's Mac," she said, recognizing immediately a photograph of their lively Australian friend. "Is he in the show or something?"

"Read the title!" hissed Moira.

"*Cork Street Liggers List,*" read Audrey. She gasped. "What is this? Who made it?"

Moira was too stunned to respond. She pointed to the italicized sub-heading.

Look out for these jokers at Private Views, and inform them that their company is not required.

"My God," breathed Audrey, flicking through the pages. "There's Bonnie, 'number five' - they've numbered them - and Richard, 'number three' - well he is a bloody wino, even I'll say that. Hey, how the hell did they get these mug shots?"

"They must have taken them zooming in on their phones or something," said Moira, disturbed. "How creepy is that?"

"It's like the... Most Unwanted list!" hissed Audrey.

"Well, if Richard's number three, who on earth is number one?" said Audrey, taking off her glasses and squinting at the offending document. She slowly turned it back to the front page.

"Excuse me!" a young woman dressed in crisp designer attire appeared before the two friends. Her blond hair had been carefully teased into a deliberately scruffy bun, clipped and sprayed into place. Without a further word she snatched the list out of their hands. "This is not for you," she said coldly before turning on her heel and disappearing into a back room.

"Well, we've really stirred up the hornet's nest now," said Moira, shaking her head. "I think we should get out of here."

Audrey nodded slowly. The pair abandoned their empty glasses on the counter and exited, making their way through the crowd that had spilled out onto the street.

"Bill Brown is on 'til nine," said Audrey. "We can go there... far away from Big Brother gallery."

"We weren't on that list were we?" asked Moira.

"Well we only saw the first couple of pages but I doubt it," replied Audrey confidently. "We're not really like the others."

Simon

Pandora Ash was now a very famous pop singer. She'd started out singing about Freud at artists' studio parties when she was only fifteen.

A couple of years later, in 2007, she had been spotted and signed to MEGA label, but it wasn't until 2011 that she launched her first EP. The label had been waiting for the 'right moment', and it seems that right moment had been the height of the vintage fashion craze.

Pandora had always been dressed head to foot in old-fashioned clothing, and during that painful four year wait she continued to wow small gatherings across the East End with a pillar box hat or a tightly fitted sailor suit, her bright red hair pinned into all kinds of rolls and folds.

Everybody was blown away by her soulful voice and interesting, witty songs. Pandora would stick about after her set, mixing with artists, liggers, poets and activists. "When the label pulls their finger out I'm gunna have you all perform on my tracks," she regularly pledged.

However, when the label finally summoned her to the studios she found she didn't have much say on these matters, in fact she didn't really even get to make her own music at all. On the up side, the label had been very supportive of her style, and she was always urged to appear in the most outrageous, daring, and ultra-retro attire.

When she performed at the Baftas last month she wore a golden turban with the most enormous peacock feather and was suspended in mid-air on a chaise longue in a shimmering gold smoking suit. As a result of her 'bold' styling, she was known, not so much for her music, as for her look.

***

During fashion week the designer shops in Bond Street were open late, serving gallons of champagne in an attempt to intoxicate the masses into buying their merch. The liggers were out in force.

In Ralph Lauren, Simon Baldwin was topped up by an attentive shop assistant.

"Oh you are kind," he beamed, moving down the staircase and flicking his satin scarf over his shoulder as he went. Below he could see the unmistakable form of his friend Richard, prowling around the shop floor in his illegal Siberian wolf fur coat.

"Oh there you are, you old slag," said Simon as he reached the ground.

"I went to Cork Street," said Richard, his mass of frizzy curls beaming in the bright shop lights. "But I don't know what's going on down there, they told me to leave at practically every private view I went to."

"I had that," snapped Simon. "I popped into Simon Taylor Gallery – just for a tipple after my diabolical interview at the Job Centre – and the little prick at the desk asked me if I was buying anything. I said 'well how do I know when I've not even seen the bloody art?' Then he steps onto the street and says 'I think you'd better come out'. I said 'I came out in 1975 doll face, when are you going to come out?'". Simon screamed, clapped his hands together and threw his head back with laughter.

Richard was not amused. "Janine Bruce had the same experience. She said that she went to Bill Brown's and they immediately told her that the private view was only for collectors and that she clearly wasn't there to buy anything."

"Beasts!" shrieked Simon.

"Something's going on," continued Richard. "I mean, how do they know?"

"Oh you're just being paranoid," said Simon. "It's probably that coat. I mean is it really necessary to go round like the Queen of Narnia? It's only September."

"Oh find out for yourself then," snarled Richard, turning on his heel. "I'm going to G.A.Y."

"Ohhhh, can I come?"

But Richard was already inside the revolving door. His fur coat was momentarily pressed up against the glass like a hamster scurrying around in a perspex ball, and then he was off into the night.

Simon, alone again, spotted two familiar faces pass the shop and he plonked his champagne glass on an empty mannequin stand. "Come on! Come on!" he barked to the doors as they spun round slowly, impeding the frustrated ligger.

"Bitches!" he screamed, leaping onto the pavement.

Moira and Audrey, his two faithful drinking friends, stopped in their tracks and turned around.

Simon raced towards them and flung his arms around them; they laughed, rejoicing at the reunion.

"Where are we going?" Simon asked excitedly bouncing up and down on the spot.

"Well, we've given up on Cork Street so we decided to try some of the fashion week parties."

"What's going on with Cork Street? Is it true all this crap about everybody being thrown out of galleries?" asked Simon.

"Yes... it's the list," said Audrey.

"What list?" Simon's eyebrows were raised in two black points, like a giant M across his face.

"Oh, haven't you heard? Moira and I found a list of 'Cork Street Liggers' in the Albatross Gallery," sighed

Audrey wearily.

"You're fucking joking!" squawked Simon.

"I'm fucking not," said Audrey standing up straight, her stocky frame formed a short rectangle. "It's been circulated. Liggers are now lepers.'

"He was right," said Simon quietly.

"Who?" said Audrey.

"Oh just Richard, he thought something was up. I told him he was mad and he stormed off in a huff. Anyway, never mind, I'm sure he's fine. He's probably got some sixteen year old school boy to lick his nipples somewhere," Simon cackled riotously and Audrey and Moira shook their heads before reluctantly chuckling along. "Unlike poor me." He added, letting out a deafening scream.

"Right," said Moira clapping her hands together, eager to crush the unsavoury image of Richard and the school boy. "Apparently some fashion magazine's having a party just off Sloane Square. All the celebrities are going."

"Oh that's fucking miles away. How are we going to get in there anyway? Are we going to dig a tunnel? Parachute out of a helicopter?"

"Where there's a will there's a way," said Audrey brightly. "We all got into the Charlie's party last week."

"Oh yes, I heard Peter Corbitt pretended to be some big wig. How dumb are they?"

"As dumb as the door whores are going to be at this party," said Moira.

***

As the three liggers neared the venue they found themselves impeded by a scrum of photographers and they stood on their tiptoes catching a glimpse of red carpet as they did so.

Suddenly an old-fashioned, sparkling white Aston Martin pulled up and a familiar face rose up from one of the doors.

"Well, will you look who it is!" gasped Simon as an elegant figure stepped onto the red carpet.

"Pandora!" yelled the paparazzi.

"Well, an old friend is exactly what we needed tonight, eh?" squeaked Simon excitedly, the faint hope of getting into the bash was becoming an achievable reality. "You remember Pandora, don't you?"

"Oh yes, from studio parties. She's very famous now," said Moira.

"Duh!" snapped Simon. "Right, all we've got to do is say we're Pandora's guests. If they bother to go and ask her she'll just say yes... she loves us, remember..."

***

Pandora smiled broadly at the cameras. Her head felt a little heavy, as she stood there beaming. She had expressed a wish to wear a rose in her hair that evening, but of course the stylist had exaggerated to the max and she now stood on the red carpet sporting a bouquet on the side of her head. She had often tilted her head to the side for photos but tonight it hung readily to the right.

She felt like a big doll rather than an artist but she was loving all the fame. She waved and picked up the bottom of her magenta ball gown and headed to the doors.

"Oooh I'm dying for a wee!" she squealed at the middle-aged door man.

He cackled sycophantically and she momentarily reflected on how down to earth she still was. She still spoke to the people. She was the same old Pandora from Bow.

"My parents and some rellies gunna pop by in a bit. Can you let 'em in for me?"

The door man smiled, his cheeks had become a deep pink. "Of course Pandora."

"Oh you ledge!" she smiled, touching his arm.

"Ladies is down the corridor..." the door man managed to give her a little wink, before his face burned into a crimson furnace.

Pandora followed her female assistant, Freddie, down the corridor and into the toilets where she contemplated her reflection in horror. She looked ridiculous.

Freddie, dressed in a neat black suit, was busily inspecting a document on her iPad. "Okay Pandora," she whispered. "I've got the guest list. Who would you like to talk to tonight?"

"Oh God, no-one with this thing on my head," she replied.

"You look stunning Pandora. Kooky. Fun. Larger than life. You're Lady GaGa, but vintage. A really great brand," Freddie said.

Pandora slumped against the hand drier. "Thanks."

The pair left the bathroom and moved into a huge, darkly-lit room where a topless man painted gold offered Pandora an apple.

"It's a Boutique Ball theme, Pandora," said Freddie informatively.

"Yes," sighed Pandora. She was always invited to these 'off-the-wall' events. Pandora's mood soon lifted as international models and fellow pop stars flocked towards her, arms swung out, and double kisses galore. These exclusive little congregations did give her a real buzz, they were the new generation of A-listers. It was so exciting!

"Ohhhhh, hello Shoreditch set. Can I please photograph you?" said Camilla, Fashion Editor of *Gracias* Magazine.

"Babes, I love your song 'Please'. It's just so beautiful, I actually cried," cooed Candice, one of Pandora's pop contemporaries, in reference to her latest smash hit.

Candice placed a hand on her heart and launched into the chorus: 'Please don't break my heart again. I don't think I can get back up again, if you dooooo.'

As Pandora continued to revel in her new friendships, she became aware of a tapping on her arm.

Suddenly a face assembled itself in her vision. It was an older male face, framed by grey straggly curls. It looked as though these curls may have been scraped back at some point during the evening but now they cascaded freely over his glasses, underneath which two magnified blue eyes stared out.

There was a sense of mania about this person, his black eyebrows were raised into two ninety degree points, and he was grinning with such force that Pandora thought the sides of his mouth might split. She suddenly felt afraid.

"Hello you!" he sung.

"He-llo," tremmered Pandora.

Freddie was immediately by her side. "Who are you?" she enquired assertively.

"I'm an old friend of Pandora's thank you. Who are you?"

"Pandora?" said Freddie, with obvious concern.

Suddenly Pandora had a flashback of dancing with this man, and a couple of other bedraggled individuals in an antique shop in Stepney. It had been a poetry evening and she had sung her song 'See ya later Oedipus'.

Afterwards, they drank absinthe and someone had poppers, of all things. They had bayed cockney tunes till six in the morning, high as kites.

"That was a right knees up," murmured Pandora in a daze of recollection.

The man screamed louder than a thousand sirens and clapped his hands. "Those were the days!" he whooped hysterically.

Pandora cringed, the realisation of her present surroundings re-emerging. Candice and her people were edging away, while Freddie was poised behind her, gearing up for interception.

"Well, we have to thank you for getting us into this fabulous party," continued the man, by now vibrating with excitement.

"Me?" squeaked Pandora.

"Yes my dear. We just said we were with you and in we came. Oh, you remember Audrey and Moira, don't you?" the man moved to the side revealing two frumpy elderly ladies who grinned and waved.

It suddenly dawned on Pandora exactly what had happened at the door. "Er, yes… hello," she said faintly.

The three gate-crashers moved in to hover around her, swooping up Camparis, now perfectly at home it seemed.

They thanked her relentlessly, joking how good she was to help out her old chums. They also revealed (extremely loudly) how they were no longer allowed into the galleries of Cork Street as a result of some kind of blacklisting. Pandora stood mute and helpless.

"I still remember your song about the boy who couldn't stop masturbating," trilled Moira, twisting some mini kebabs into tissues and stuffing them in her bag. There was a collective gasp from the crowd that surrounded them, and she heard Candice let out a high pitched giggle.

Pandora found herself wishing somebody could actually have a heart attack or something to end this excruciating ordeal.

"This. Is. Not. Good... ," hissed Freddie in her ear. Her team had spent a lot of money mine-sweeping YouTube for videos of such performances.

Strangely Pandora felt a brief wave of nostalgia as she stood with the liggers. She had been just like them once, finding boundless joy in warm company and free booze. But it was different now. She didn't have to stand about in old bookshops anymore with a load of crazy artists. She had her fame and fortune and an invitation to any party she wanted.

She had worked hard for this and she wasn't going to let a few losers bring her down. What had that fixation with Freud and Jung been about anyway? It had all just been a really embarrassing phase.

"I don't know them," she hissed at Freddie, before turning away from the trio. She looked at Candice and mouthed 'HELP!' Candice threw back her head with laughter and linked Pandora's arm, easing her away.

"I think they're fans or something," shrugged Pandora as they sailed off into the party.

***

"So… Pandora Ash is a huge fat sell out!" spat Audrey as the three friends made their way down Kings Road.

"Oh well, we got to have a good few drinks, eh?" said Simon cheerily. "She's a silly girl but we should use her name more often. It worked a treat didn't it? I have to say I do miss all the art... these celeb parties are so boring.

But anyway, beggars can't be choosers."

"Hey, we could use that Candice's name too," mused Moira. "Technically we know her as well after tonight. We're going to need all the help we can get while this liggers list's about."

"Yes, well you are number eight Simon," said Audrey.

"Is that it? Number eight! I'm insulted. Who's number one?"

"We don't know. We were rudely interrupted before we could find out… "

Mac, Grettil and Peter Corbitt

Grettil lay back in the bath of her Clapton flat and looked up at the ceiling. Large lines penetrated the plaster and she hoped it wasn't the mama of all degenerative diseases - subsidence.

She reached into the bubbles, and retrieved Bertha. She began to wash her with the sponge, reflecting on the textural difference between Bertha's skin and her own. The smooth tan-coloured shiny plastic against her own soft pale dimples was fascinating, she mused. This contemplation charged Grettil with a bolt of inspiration.

She would move forward with new art projects, she vowed, although her mood hadn't permitted her to do so for a while. It was Up. Down. Up Down. London. Berlin, London Berlin. Bed. Private View. Bed. Private View. Bed.

She washed her own skin. Like the ceiling, it was not what it used to be, travelling further with each stroke than even the last time she bathed. But she was not one for caring about such things. Ageing was fascinating to Grettil.

She would make a whole video of her skin and of the bathroom ceiling, she decided. She'd show it in Hackney and in Kreuzberg. Her mood darkened. Last time she had exhibited in Kreuzberg she had shown a collection of her dirty laundry on a clothes horse. It had certainly attracted a lot of attention in the local press, but within months a near identical art work was erected in a pristine, white-painted, top London gallery, provoking a feverish 'is it art?' debate and rocketing its creator into the orbit of international stardom... Grettil's clothes horse was completely forgotten.

Grettil felt irritating tickles of bitterness slide into her throat and took deep, meditative breaths. She would not let herself think about Stacey Lenin. It was dangerous territory.

She racked her brain for a distraction. *What was on tonight?*

Grettil remembered there was a group performance at Cunt Gallery, a small artist-run space in Hackney. It was curated by Mark Camp, the radical video artist. She rinsed Bertha under the tap and popped her over the side of the bath, placing her on the pale green bathmat. Next, Dominik. Her little boy was getting old too... you could barely see the paint on his face anymore. She was careful not to scrub him too thoroughly. Once she had bathed all her dolls she lovingly wrapped them in flannels and stood up herself. Her phone was ringing in the other room - that tinny X-Files ring tone. She remembered the man in a basement shop in Homerton pulling it out of a bin bag full of old phones - all stolen no doubt.

She stepped out of the bath and into the commodious living room but did not venture towards the dreary trill. It was probably Mac - the drunk yet rather attractive Australian she had met at the Marvin Pailey Gallery - wondering if she was coming to trail hopelessly round Mayfair; she had received a voicemail from him earlier that day stating he 'strongly suspected' that there was an exciting private view on Park Lane. "The artist's website states that the show opens to the public tomorrow," Mac had explained. He was certainly open about his intentions. This was no closeted gatecrasher... "Nine times out of ten the Private View is the night before it goes public," he went on to insist to her voicemail box.

She, however, was completely uninterested in conversing with liggers. Sure, she had friends in the East

End who liked a freebie, who you may call a ligger for a laugh. But these were all artists, too devoted to their creative pursuits to put hand to mouth. These West End liggers were... a new, more aggressive strand entirely.

Grettil lit a Vogue menthol cigarette and looked in the mirror of her dresser. Her enormous hazel eyes stared back from a thick mask of foundation make-up, a canvas on which she decided to smudge black eye shadow both across her eyelids and a good centimetre underneath. She loved the panda-eyed look, especially with her big glassy stare... haunting.

Her Nanna had always said her eyes were 'thyroidy,' which she took to mean that they bulged. And they did bulge, they were amphibious - protruding out of her skull with that watery glaze.

They were like... turtle eggs, she thought remembering the documentary she had watched late last night about the giant turtles of the Great Barrier Reef.

She laughed out loud at the thought of her eyes resembling such things, a seductive throaty laugh, exhaling upwards a spiral of smoke. She was not one for vanity, she wanted her very being to be living and breathing art and thus, any quirks in her anatomy were very much welcome.

She applied more foundation, the desired effect being that of an alabaster mannequin. "Brings out your eyes more," she giggled manically to her reflection.

Having applied her makeup, she looked up at her wig collection, stacked on top of a mannequin like a big, rainbow, hairy tower of Pisa - there were pinks, silvers, coppers. What mood was she in? A dark one, as usual.

She snatched a navy blue wig out from beneath the stack, placed it to her forehead and threw back her head waiting for the nylon strands to settle around her shoulders. She stood in front of the mirror, drawing heavily from her cigarette weighing up the full effect.

"For fuck's sake" she muttered grabbing some scissors. She looked like she was off to buy Doc Martins in Camden. She started hacking into the wig, leaving one side long and one side short; she attacked the fringe too, chopping it into a straight block. *Tolerable.*

The phone rang again and she slid it open impatiently. "Ja?"

"Hello! Gretta, it's Mac here, the guy who you were talking to at Marvin Paileys."

"Ja?" snapped Grettil again brushing away snippets of hair that clung to her nightdress.

"Well, hey did you get my message earlier?"

"Ja..." sighed Grettil.

"Oh okay. So you're busy tonight?" Mac persisted.

"Ja."

"Right, well what are you doing? Because we went to the show I mentioned earlier, and I don't know what happened, but they threw us out after about five minutes."

Grettil raised a painted eyebrow and lit another Vogue. "I am going to Cunt Gallery."

"Oh, wow. Where's that?" Mac enthused.

"Hackney," exhaled Grettil.

"Right, fantastic. And what's showing there?" pressed Mac.

He was not easily deterred.

"A group show curated by Mark Camp, the video artist. You may have heard of him, he explores incest a lot in his work?" Grettil was sure this would get rid of him.

There was a silence. "Hmmm, and will there be wine and food?"

"Wine sure, but I doubt food," Grettil replied, exhaling wearily.

"Okay," said Mac his voice picking up a little. "Well, I'm just with my friends Peter and Deborah now so I'll see if they want to come. What's the address?"

"56 Graham Road," Grettil replied and she snapped shut the phone. She did not want to be seen with these West London piranhas devouring everything in sight. She glugged from a bottle of vodka and angrily applied another layer of foundation. She would completely ignore them when they arrived.

She sat at her dresser lacing up her PVC ankle boots, and then she made her way to the front door, throwing a coat over her silk nightdress and popping on her large Russian pilot cap.

Grettil marched down Clapton High Street, bumping straight into any hipsters that crossed her path. She was still angry that Clapton had become 'cool,' that these sheep in tight trousers had to flock where artists had happily dwelled for years. It made her want to pack up and go back to Germany.

Just before she reached Hackney Central, she cut down a dark side street where a group of smokers outside a building indicated an event was underway.

Upon entering the Cunt Gallery she immediately saw a video of a girl in purple stilettos giving an old man a lap dance.

"That's supposed to be her uncle in real life," came a voice in the darkness next to her.

"Oh really... how *avant garde*," she hissed back venomously, and the shadow slipped away.

She squinted across the darkly lit room. Her ex-lover, the poet Phillip G. Hunt was standing by the wine table with that frumpy American artist. *So they're still together,* she inwardly seethed; she had assumed it would be a quick fling, after all, everybody knew the yank was only using him for a visa.

She watched them for a moment; the American was taller than the greying five feet, six inches Phillip G. Hunt and was hunching over to say something in his ear. His gaze caught her own and he quickly looked away.

Guilt, fumed Grettil.

Phillip knew she still bore strong feeling for him, she had told him as much last month on a canal boat party when the American was in New York. And here he was, parading his fraudulent relationship in front of her.

She stormed across the room, her tall thin silhouette cutting a menacing shape in the pilot hat and bondage boots. Her mind raged. *Show Time! She would cut off his -*

To her fury, the pair disappeared into another dark room and just like that, Grettil was suddenly unable to cope with the whole scene. She retreated, turning on her heel and marching back across the room and out onto the street where she searched her bag frantically for Vogues.

The X-Files tone whistled in her pocket and she flipped open the phone, shoving it between her shoulder and cheek.

"What the fuck do you want?" she screamed.

"Gretta, I can't hear you very well, we're in a pub, it's very noisy," came Mac's response. "Anyway, just to let you know, we're actually going to stay around Cork Street. I've just found out there's a party at Charlie's tonight, and we're definitely going to get in. We'd love you to come, I think you'll have a great time."

Grettil was silent. She found these people's desperation to scrounge from the elite art world really quite detestable, but now her nerves were on razor edge she

needed a distraction, one away from the East End at that.
"I'm coming," she snapped, sauntering down the backstreets towards the bright lights of Mare Street.

***

"Hey, I must introduce you to Peter," said Mac, nodding his head at the pasty, wiry man at the bar, dressed in a poorly fitted suit, like that of a school boy.
"No, it's okay," sighed Grettil.
They stood in a pub in the backstreets of Green Park, adjacent to Cork Street, where many mainstream galleries were located.
"Well, I'm glad you decided to come along," said Mac cheerfully looking Grettil up and down. "You look good and you've got a new hair style I see?"
"Uh-huh," Grettil inhaled tensely, but as she looked up at Mac she felt herself defrost a little. She had been in an erratic mood ever since the Cunt Gallery but Mac was so kind and relentlessly easy-going Grettil couldn't help but like him. "So where are we going?"
"Oh just a pre-auction party at *Charlie's*. Peter's got good contacts there," said Mac.
Grettil looked back over to the bar just as Peter blew his nose on his sleeve.
"Ja?" she winced.
After sharing a poisonous glass of plonk, Grettil followed them outside the pub where another of Mac's insalubrious acquaintances named Meryl was lurching about on the pavement, clearly drunk already. Mac was quick to invite her along.
During the walk, Meryl shed light on the source of her intoxication: a funeral that afternoon of a fellow ligger's

distant relative. After an eternity, they reached the famous auction house where, to Grettil's astonishment, the doormen unclipped the rope for Peter ahead of a queue that stretched down the street and around the corner.

The five shuffled into the grand, spacious foyer where an immaculate Asian lady glided downstairs towards them, arms spread out, with an air of obvious excitement.

"Mr Schwartz!" she cried, kissing a flushed Peter on both cheeks.

"Hello," said Peter. "You remember Mac and Deborah? Well, I've also brought along Meryl, my assistant, and the emerging Berlin Artist, Grettil… er?

"Bretton," said Grettil through clenched teeth. *What on earth was this cretin doing?*

"Anyway, everyone this is Violette, Head of Contemporary Sales," Peter concluded, proudly.

Violette's eyes travelled from Grettil's pilot hat down to her silk nightdress, expressing evident distaste, before breaking into a smile. "How wonderful, what a pleasure, Grettil."

"I am so delighted to see you all... ," she placed a finely manicured hand on Peter's arm. "Your people said you were coming!"

"My people?" croaked Peter.

"Yes," said Violette, and then she lowered her voice and whispered just loud enough for Grettil to hear. "By the way, we are expecting the Hurst series to break all records. We are delighted you chose to place it with us..."

***

Peter was euphorically sinking his teeth into a mini grilled chicken-burger when he felt a tap on his shoulder.

He turned to find Violette Wu smiling broadly, her pearl white teeth almost as dazzling as the chandeliers that blazed above them. He moved his mouth to greet her but remembered his mouth was full and so he made some 'hello' sounding noises whilst pointing to his bulging cheeks.

"Mr Schwartz, I am so sorry to disturb you while you're enjoying our hospitality but may I please introduce you to Signor Pedro Barbieri?" she gracefully stepped aside to reveal a short and stout Mediterranean looking man, dressed in tails with a paisley handkerchief in his pocket. His black hair was scraped over his balding head like tar streaked across a big terracotta ball.

Peter gulped down his burger but before he could open his mouth, Signor Barbieri was pumping his hand excitedly.

"Mr Schwartz, what a joy to meet you. Your fine eye is notorious across the continent," he boomed, his voice surprisingly deep and husky for a man of his height.

Peter let out a squeak as his hand moved limply within the powerful squeeze of Signor Barbieri's chubby fingers.

"If my sources aren't mistaken, I hear you currently possess the crown jewels of contemporary art... ," Mr Barbieri and Violette threw back their heads, clapped their hands together and laughed in manic artificial wonder.

"Oh. I try," muttered Peter, scouring the room urgently for means of escape.

"So modest, Mr Schwartz," said Signor Barbieri .

Violette touched an arm of each gracefully, grinning from ear to ear: "Gentlemen, if you'll excuse me," she said, before slipping into the crowd.

"Now, Mr Schwartz, I shall bore you no longer with this tedious flattery. I'm sure you would also prefer if I were to cut straight to the point," Signor Barbieri said, suddenly leaning towards him with what could only be described as a menacing stance.

"Hmm?" exhaled Peter, eyes as wide as saucers.

Signor Barbieri lowered his voice into a steely murmur: "I have a meticulously placed source who informs me that the Hurst series will not, after all, be for sale in the auction tomorrow."

"Hmm?" Peter squeaked.

"In fact my source tells me that at the auction tomorrow, there will be an announcement stating that the collector has withdrawn the pieces, and wishes to keep them after all. But we all know what that means, don't we, Mr Schwartz?"

Peter could no longer muster any suitable sound-effects and he began to take a step backwards.

"You see, my - erm - shall we say... team - have flown in from Sicily to secure that fine series of paintings. The boss has got his heart set on them... "

Peter looked behind him, seeking an exit, but only found a sharp white corner, the ninety degree union of two closed walls.

"Oh... right," he said looking over Signor Barbieri 's shoulder trying to catch Deborah or Martin's eye. They, however, were completely intoxicated by the champagne stand and incapable of seeing past their glasses.

"The Boss doesn't like to be disappointed, Mr Schwartz, and I am sure you wouldn't like him to take his disappointment out on me... " he paused and leaned even closer in, "... or you -"

Peter let out a terrified giggle. "Oh!" he squeaked.

Signor Barbieri's face relaxed and he broke into hearty laughter, slapping Peter on the back: "So... we have an understanding?"

"Hmmm," tremmered Peter.

"Now, as this is all a bit, er, what do you British say... behind the table? No, below - below the table," Signor Barbieri laughed before continuing. "Anyway, I don't think it is in either of our interests to have this conversation played out across our bank statements, wouldn't you say?"

Peter stood in a stunned silence as Signor Barbieri reached into a hand-stitched pocket and then slipped something into Peter's own, nylon, blazer pocket. "Have a feel, Mr Schwartz," he said winking and checking around him.

Peter put his hand in his pocket and felt a small ridged metal object.

"How would you feel about a top of the range, luxury yacht to seal the deal? Prowls and purrs across the ocean like a black jaguar. Sleeps ten, mini ballroom, double decks," Signor Barbieri raised a thick black eyebrow, like a question mark. "She's sitting waiting for you in Chioggia, dock number 573," he leaned closer and hissed. "Registered to nobody, worth £3 million."

Peter let out another nervous giggle and in turn, Signor Barbieri threw back his head and let out another howl of laughter.

"Pleasure doing business with you," he smiled before adding, "My people will talk to Charlie's for you and settle any, er... outstanding costs with Mademoiselle Wu. You need do nothing more... ."

As soon as Signor Barbieri's back was turned, Peter leapt into action, grabbing the nearest glass of champagne and drinking it in two or three gulps. He plunged into crowd, bristling through the fur coats towards the bar where Alexia, Deborah and Meryl were now gently swaying in contrasting directions.

"We've got to go!" he spluttered grabbing another champagne.

"What do you mean? This is *Charlie's*!" slurred Deborah, now cross-eyed.

"We're going to get found out. I should never have shown that bloody card. Let's go," Peter hissed before throwing himself back into the sea of fur. The liggers sighed before finishing their drinks and following with deep reluctance. They weaved their way to the door, Meryl staggering behind, using guests' arms to assist her. They finally arrived on the stairs just as Violette Wu was ascending.

She placed her white glove on Peter's arm: "Oh Mr Schwartz, just who I was looking for! Signor Barbieri informs me that you have had *a very interesting conversation*," she purred in tones laden with suggestion. "I just wanted to check with you that you are happy with arrangements?" Peter stared at her helplessly, then nodded, unable to speak.

"Well I'm delighted we could help... good night then, Mr Schwartz" smiled Violette, gathering her gown and continuing up the staircase.

As the line of confused and grumpy liggers filed down the stairs they could see a scene erupting in the foyer between a slender bespectacled gentleman and a lady with the guest list.

"Oh hey, that's that Schwartz guy we were talking about the other night," slurred Alexia. Peter stopped in his tracks and they all crashed into each other.

"Up the stairs! Up the stairs!," he hissed and they turned and scampered back into the auction rooms.

***

As Grettil and Mac roamed the cavernous navy blue rooms, Grettil whistled in awe. The art was impressive: decapitated mannequins hung from the ceiling; Richard Princes and Warhols tiled the walls, there were also Richters, Hirsts, Kosamas, Lichtensteins. How these four liggers had blagged their way in here she did not know.

"You have actually impressed me," she said to Mac truthfully.

"Fantastic collection, eh?" said Mac, guzzling down some champagne to make way for the top up that was on offer. Grettil held out her own glass to the waiter and the pair quickly found themselves debating the merits of a Hirst sculpture in front of them.

"I want to just chop off his hands," snapped Grettil, as Mac enthused over the piece.

Mac cut short his praise. "I guess he's the Marmite of art," he said cheerily.

Grettil had to admire Mac. She could be a little frightening, yes, but he always carried on happy as Larry... She felt her heart flutter for a moment, and realised she had not experienced such a sensation since Phillip G. Hunt. Mac leaned in to whisper in Grettil's ear and she leaned closer, suddenly breathless with anticipation.

"Wow!" breathed Mac. "You're not going to believe this, but Stacey Lenin has just walked in."

The fluttering in Grettil's heart quickly transformed into heavy pounding, like that of a cold steel drum. She turned slowly to see that her nemesis had, indeed, entered the room and was heading in their direction.

****

"The fire exit!" shouted Peter.

They pushed through the crowds, grabbing cocktails as they went. "Mr Schwartz!" bellowed a familiar voice as they skidded past. Peter could see Signor Barbieri standing with a crowd of grinning Sicilians out of the corner of his eye. They looked like something straight out of *The Godfather*. Peter kept his head down and continued.

"We'll never be allowed into *Charlie's* again," he whimpered as they searched frantically for the fire exits.

"There he is!" screamed a familiar French accent. Peter looked up to see Violette Wu, pointing a finger at him from the main entrance, her ordinarily glorious smile now transformed into a thunderous black scowl.

Peter yelped as he saw three burley security guards ascend the stairs and head in their direction.

"Oh my giddy aunt!" Peter cried. "Oh, my giddy aunt!" he cried again, louder.

"Oh, don't tell me I'm supposed to run away from them now?" shouted Meryl collapsing into Deborah. The crowds began to part, nervously, allowing the guards to advance.

Suddenly there was a crash in the corner of the room. Peter looked over, and to his amazement he could see that the strange German woman Mac had brought along had pinned somebody up against the wall.

"Is that Stacey Lenin?" gaped Deborah.

As they craned their necks and stood on their tip-toes they could make out a pilot's hat looming over the unmistakable face of British contemporary art.

"You are so full of shit!" they heard Grettil scream.

"You are so FULL of shit," they heard again.

And then - "thief!"

To Peter's great relief, the security guards turned in their tracks and rushed over to rescue their prestigious guest. Violette Wu trailed behind them, pale and aghast, as though she might collapse.

The group crept through the crowd - which was now migrating to the scene of the disturbance - and burst through the fire doors, down the stairs and out into the refreshing chill of the winter's night.

Half an hour later, they had safely returned to the sanctity of The Kings Head in the backstreets of Mayfair. After pooling their change they bought a bottle of the cheapest white wine and Peter sat in stunned silence as he drank the misty putrid substance, letting the evening's events sink in.

Half an hour later, they were joined by Mac and an elated, hatless Grettil.

"I've been waiting twenty years to do that," she smiled.

"You were like something out of Alien!" said Mac warily.

Grettil threw back her head and laughed - a scary throaty cackle - before perching on a stall and tugging her wig back into place.

Peter looked pensively around the table at his fellow liggers and dreamers. "Where exactly is Chioggia?" he asked.

William, Ashpak and Tony Phun

"I absolutely hate those two artists, they are just so morose... and sickly," William grimaced, and every wrinkle in his face was activated, like a big, scrunched up piece of paper. "Their art is morose! It's morose goo!"

"Uh-huh, uh-huh,' Ashpak, the stout Indian scientist was now nodding along, despite having praised the 'morose' duo just seconds before.

"What I particularly hate is that thing they made with the pile of rubbish, where it's actually a big sculpture of their faces," William continued, unwittingly resembling the very spectacle itself. His tone was tense and clipped, as though constipated, and now only the whites of his eyes could be seen. As he had rolled them they had become momentarily stuck, so intense was his scorn.

"Oh yeah, I know the one you mean, I saw that in 2007 - ," began Ashpak.

"It just makes me want to dismember them and arrange their arms and legs into a big heap, and say 'oh look this is *actually* a sculpture of a beautiful swan'," snarled William, swirling the merlot in the glass, his irises now visible again and gleaming with contempt.

"Mmm. Mmm. Yeah," Ashpak joined in, smiling unsurely.

They were at a private view in Albermale Street in the West End; photographs were hung around the white walls in straight lines - a series of a naked man doing his shopping.

Ashpak caught sight of a male gallery assistant circulating in the background, clutching a piece of paper to his chest. Ashpak's smile faded. "Oh blimey," he mumbled, looking down. "It's the list".

"Oh that thing we're all on, that identifies us as scroungers void of interest in anything other than booze and nibbles?" William twitched, and his greying brown bob flicked around his ears.

"Yeah," said Ashpak, nervously, sneaking an upwards glance. "Here we go..."

The gallery assistant stopped before them. He was a tidy individual who wore black skinny jeans and patent lace-up shoes with no socks. A chunky crucifix pendant hung over his sleeveless t-shirt and his hair was carefully blow-dried into a sort-of-bouffant.

"Excuse me Sir, but I've been watching you both all night, and you really haven't looked at the art once," he began, launching into a speech that the liggers had become all too accustomed to. The surrounding groups of elite guests fell silent and looked on at William and Ashpak with suspicion.

"That's because it's shit," said William abruptly, knocking back his drink.

The man blinked. A snigger could be heard and he flushed pink momentarily before attempting to regain control.

"Excuse me?"

"It's shit."

"Well, if you feel that way, Sir, then perhaps you'd like to leave," he said defiantly.

"Well, no, I don't want to leave actually. I want another drink."

"That's not possible I'm afraid," said the assistant brightly, lifting his arm in the direction of the door. As he did so the piece of paper flapped about in his hand.

"What's that then?" snapped William. "A warrant for my arrest?"

"No, it's just the guest list," he smiled bitchily, "...the

one that you're not on."

"I think we both know that's not true," said William, his voice dripping with cynicism. "It's your stupid little index of human beings who come to fill your otherwise sterile space, and, on arrival, need to drown their sorrows over the downfall of British culture."

The assistant was clearly not accustomed to such sustained resistance and fingered his crucifix nervously, looking around for back-up, which was not forthcoming.

"Now, you've bored me to death with your horrible nudes," finished William, combing his hand nonchalantly through his bob. "So just give me some fucking wine."

***

Ashpak and William found themselves out on the street within minutes of the latter's outburst.

"Look, William," said Ashpak. "I'm not sure we should necessarily be biting back like that."

"Why not? Are we just going to let them dehumanize us? Make us anonymous like some kind of art vermin?" asked William.

"You have to just play their little game if you want to drink at their galleries."

"Well, you do."

"Okay, well obviously you do too. Do you have anywhere else for us to go now?"

William was silent.

"That was the only thing, unless you want to go all the way to Victoria? There's a tiny gallery opening there."

"Well, we'll have to walk."

"It'll be over by the time we get there if we walk. Look, I can lend you the Oyster fare."

Ashpak and William walked glumly through the back streets towards Piccadilly. They attempted to make conversation but a sense of dejection hung in the air and their half-hearted chatter soon fizzled out.

As they turned the corner by the Kings Head, the compact figure of Tony Phun came into view. He carried a floppy leather brief case and walked calmly towards them.

"Hi Tony," said Ashpak, his voice picking up despite their gloom. Tony Phun was renowned for getting into events.

"Hello," said Tony coolly. He wore the same blue velvet blazer and polka-dot dickie bow that he wore every evening. He nodded at William.

"So, where are you going Tony?" asked Ashpak, getting straight to the point.

"New Bond Street," Tony replied.

"Oh wow, what's happening there?" asked Ashpak excitedly, crossing his arms and leaning in.

"A Hotel party," Tony Phun answered through lips stained with red wine - also a trademark feature.

"Oh right, wow. So what kind of Hotel party?" quizzed Ashpak.

"Four Seasons"

"Uh-huh, and is it invite only?" Ashpak persevered.

"Yes."

Tony raised a hand to wave them goodnight.

"Can we come?" Ashpak shouted after him. But he was gone.

"So, what's his secret?" said Ashpak, dejectedly. "I mean, I see that guy coming out of the hostel around the corner from me every morning, he obviously lives there, and yet he gets into all these parties. Apparently he uploaded a selfie of himself and Vivienne Westwood on

Facebook the other day..."

"Oh, have you not seen his website?" William asked, pulling out his phone and tapping some buttons. "This is great, this is."

He sighed as he waited impatiently for it to load.

"Here," he said thrusting the phone under Ashpak's nose.

"Tony Phun, Deputy Director of ..." read Ashpak slowly. "What? You are joking!"

William put the phone into his pocket. "There's no predator like a silent predator. Silent and violent."

"Can you believe the balls on that guy?" cried Ashpak.

"Mmm," agreed William.

"Deputy Director of H***** N******." said Ashpak incredulously.

"Well, maybe he can pull it off. Unlike that idiot Peter Corbitt," said William.

"Hey! Peter is my friend!" cried Ashpak. "And anyway, what are you talking about?"

"Well, your friend Peter tried to impersonate some kind of mega art dealer... Anyway, rumour has it that one thing led to another and he ended up having to do a deal with the Sicilian Mafia over some art they thought he owned..."

"Oh blinking blimey," gasped Ashpak.

"Well nobody's seen him in weeks."

"Oh blinking shitting blimey!"

"Well, it's probably because of that bloody list!" said William as they resumed their journey to Victoria. "It'll be the death of us all."

Bonnie and Reverend George

Reverend George was feeling smashed. For the past half an hour he had been sucking up the effervescent fountains of champagne that had crashed into his glass. It now appeared that these had suddenly dried up and so he undertook the mission of searching for the source itself.

The private view was set in a narrow space, almost like a corridor and heaving with gallery-goers; the drinks table had become rather hard to locate. He found himself swaying gently between Simon Baldwin and Richard. He was about to ask them for some guidance on the matter, before realising he was standing in the middle of a dispute.

"You'd better not bring that wicked old dyke back to our house," Simon was squawking. "I'll have her guts for garters if you do. And yours. And I'll move out too. Disgusting".

Reverend George sighed loudly and Simon and Richard looked up at him for a second before resuming their spat.

"Oh good, move out then. I could do with my sofa back," replied Richard dryly.

"That's fine, I'll move in with Peter. He said I could stay," Simon bit back.

"Peter's disappeared into thin air. Nobody's seen him in weeks," said Richard. "So, good luck."

Reverend George withdrew and decided that the best course of action was to move on; he had heard of a show at the Italian Institute and glancing at his watch, realised that he could probably make it there for a couple more drinks.

He was wading across the crowded room towards the

door, when he suddenly felt a tugging at his arm. Turning his head he could just about see that Bonnie McCarten had reached an arm through the throng and attached herself to his sleeve. His immediate thought was that something was wrong... he had never really spoken with Bonnie, and could not think why else she would claw at his overcoat.

He turned slowly to investigate, when, to his shock, he saw a fist snatch at his chest, and then a tremendous weight pulling at his upper body. He stood there powerless as Bonnie used the front of his cassock as leverage to haul herself through the crowd. Drinks spilt around them, as guests were knocked sideways, and Bonnie drew herself towards him with a steely relentlessness.

"What the hell?!!" came a voice from the crowd.

"Seriously?" a woman shouted, her pale clad arms and torso dripping with spilled red wine.

Reverend George let out a howl as Ms McCarten collapsed onto him - she was a big boned lady and not an airy weight to take. He quickly stepped sideways so the pair did not fall backwards, and stumbled against the open front door.

"Is something wrong, Bonnie?" asked Reverend George, stabilising himself.

"Where are you going?" Bonnie asked, ignoring his question.

"Well... I'm going to the Italian Institute," replied Reverend George, straightening the dog collar that Bonnie had managed to dislodge.

"Can I come?" she asked quickly. Her dark grey eyes weren't quite focused on him. *They seemed ablaze with a sort-of...* Reverend George could not put his finger on it... *mania, perhaps.*

"Erm... ," Reverend George wrestled briefly with his conscience. Somebody of his calling should not shun the needy but Bonnie would, undoubtedly, be on the 'liggers list'. He'd heard that it had now been circulated to every gallery and cultural centre in the West End. He stood there racking his brains for an excuse when the crowd suddenly parted and one of the Directors could be seen circulating. Reverend George made the diplomatic decision to relocate his unavoidable interaction with black-listed Bonnie - this was a particularly generous gallery and he did not want to share her fate.

"We'll have to take the tube to get there in time," he sighed.

The two champagne-chasers buttoned up their coats as they stepped out into a crisp March night. They moved quickly through the back streets of Mayfair, and largely abstained from conversation so intent were they both on reaching their destination before it went dry.

When they moved into the warmth of Hyde Park Corner tube station, Reverend George put some more money on his Oyster card.

"Do you need to top up?" he asked Bonnie as he slotted his change into the machine. A strange smile spread across Bonnie's face and she shook her head. He noted her long black hair had become stuck to the side of her face with perspiration, a result of their trek, but she did not brush it away.

Reverend George briefly contemplated asking her to come down to the abbey next Sunday. The other church-goers were a supportive bunch. His memory glided back to the last time a ligger had attended one of his services... and had returned to receive communion four times. Reverend George decided against.

"Okey dokey. Let's go!" he said, forcing himself to sound upbeat. He would not be allowed to enter the event with Bonnie, and so he figured that, with a little charm, he could somehow convince her to enter separately from him.

Bonnie and Reverend George now made their way to the ticket barriers, and Reverend George touched his Oyster on the reader. The grey plastic gates opened for him and he quickly whipped through, all too aware that the clock was ticking against them. However, as he moved he suddenly felt a bump from behind, before something pressed against his body and appeared to travel with him to the other side.

At first Reverend George was totally confused and could not work out what had connected with him, or why, for that matter. Was it some kind of a pick-pocket? He patted his coat pocket looking around for answers until his vision rested upon Bonnie's face. Her eyes gleamed and *that* smile was fixed and macabre.

"Did you just... ?" he whispered hoarsely.

Bonnie laughed, a throaty noise, almost like a gargle: "I don't have any money."

Reverend George saw a flash of red. *Who did this woman think she was coming at him from behind like that?*

"First you pounce on me from the front and now from the back!" Father George barked. "Is there some kind of magnetic force dragging you towards me this evening, or is there just something a little bit wrong with you, lady?"

Bonnie turned on her heel without a further word and stepped on the escalator, disappearing into the abyss of the underground.

"If you call yourself a lady!" he shouted after her.

Reverend George remained at ground level seething for a couple of minutes, his wispy white hair stood on edge and his eyes bulged.

He contemplated what he should do next. If he went home, he would at least avoid running into her again.

"She's bound to bloody go there now," he muttered, leaning on a railing.

"Yes, but she's not going to get in, is she?" he argued back, holding up one hand as he rationalised the situation.

Reverend George stepped decisively onto the escalator and headed towards the Piccadilly line. Why should Bonnie McCarten spoil his fun?

He had pretty much recovered from his rage as he ascended to ground level at Russell Square. He was still in good time and would certainly make it for a night cap, maybe even two.

However, as he reached the top of the escalator, an unwelcome sight greeted him. Bonnie stood silently at the barriers, grey eyes watching him like two little tadpoles. She was waiting for him.

"You are NOT coming through with me," Reverend George snapped as he passed her. She turned to follow him and he broke into a run. As he swiped the Oyster card on the reader, he looked behind and could see Bonnie getting ready to lunge.

"NO!" he shouted loudly turning to one side to shield himself from another hump.

A nearby Underground worker looked over.

Reverend George bolted through the barrier and towards the exit. He rushed up the stairs and turned his head quickly upon leaving the station to see Bonnie still safely on the other side, now being questioned. She looked up towards him suddenly and Reverend George felt a chill as her eyes bored into him.

***

Reverend George had made it to the event and had swiftly bagged himself a glass of Prosecco. As it happened, it was hosted by the Vatican - they had recently had their own pavilion at the Venice Biennale, he learned.

Reverend George found himself chatting to a couple of cardinals. *Perhaps the Church of England could assert their presence at the Biennale too*, he mused, as he listened to them boast about their Venetian successes. From what he was starting to gather, all you had to do was get a few artists of the same persuasion. There would be millions of Anglicans who could knock up a bit of art. He was beginning to feel really quite inspired. What could be more jolly than the Venice Biennale? He had heard all the tales - it was party paradise.

"Now, I do not like to, what is this phrase in England, name-drip?" began one cardinal.

"Drop" prompted Reverend George.

"Grazie, name drop...," continued the Cardinal. "I do not like to name drop, but from one Holy man to another, that, over there is the Pope's right hand man..."

"Oh!" said Reverend George, feigning interest. "Well, be sure your sins will find you out!"

The cardinals frowned.

Not a shred of humour, thought Reverend George draining his Prosecco.

"Oh, look. He is talking with one of the Curators of the Biennale," said the other Cardinal.

Reverend George's ears pricked up. "Well, I'd be very

interested in meeting this right hand man, if you'd do the honours."

***

Reverend George momentarily took time out of his conversation to marvel at how well it was all going. The Pope's chum had been conveniently distracted and he was now able to chatter away with the Biennale Curator, who appeared delighted by his suggestions. She was rummaging around in her oversized purse for 'my one last business card' to give him whilst he stood patiently, smiling on.

Suddenly his smile froze as a rotund, overbearing figure emerged in the doorway, blocking the bright glare of the chandeliers from the corridor.

He immediately looked down but Bonnie had seen them, he could tell. He felt that unmistakable burn of her stare. When he looked up again she was sauntering towards them with the exaggerated poise of a runway model.

Reverend George watched on with dread. *What madness was she to unleash on him now?*

Strangely, when she reached them, she did not stop. Instead, she circled the pair and appeared to depart again. Reverend George watched her back hopefully as it moved away from him. *Had an unlikely miracle just occurred? Had she actually understood that he was busy, engaged in important negotiations? Had she considerately decided against further disturbance?*

As she reached the door she turned her head and, worryingly, he could see an eerie smirk.

The Curator pulled out her business card triumphantly. "I knew I had one left!" she cried. Suddenly her facial expression completely transformed into one of revulsion, and she looked as though someone had punched her in the chest.

Reverend George went to ask if she was okay but as he did so he inhaled something putrid through his nostrils. The most foul smell hung around them. Reverend George had never smelt anything like it in his entire life. It was a very deep concentrated stink. It was as though it had come from the bowels of a demon.

"Excuse me," choked the lady, looking at him with horror. "I don't feel very well." She disappeared.

Reverend George looked over at the door and could see Bonnie still standing there watching the scene unravel. She cackled and then turned away again.

Reverend George whimpered as it dawned on him what had happened. The stench had been unleashed as she circled them, and the curator no doubt believed it to be him. This woman had surely been sent straight from Hell.

There was only one thing he could do - and that was what he should have done all along. Go home.

***

A couple of weeks later, Reverend George was ready to hit the town again. He had felt a little low of late and had busied himself away from the art world, even staying on late at the abbey.

On Sunday he had opened his emails concerning forthcoming Private Views and had found one too good to resist. In a forwarded invitation from Mac the Australian (which he could see had been forwarded to and from every other ligger in town) he saw that the Rupert Steiner Gallery had a party on the Thursday. This was a white collar gallery and was bound to be flowing with cocktails and wine, and of course, the canapés would be phenomenal. Reverend George had eagerly RSVP'd.

However, when he arrived at the Rupert Steiner Gallery a very worrying sight awaited him. Liggers were being chucked out left right and centre.

Meryl, the elderly lady, was being frog-marched to the door, her matted fur coat transported behind by a waiter, while Mac was arguing in the corner with gallery staff.

"I RSVP'd!" Reverend George heard him boom.

There had been nobody on the door when Reverend George had arrived. All staff appeared busy interrogating the liggers, and he had been able to walk in with no problems at all. However, he was starting to wish that he hadn't bothered.

It was only a matter of time, he thought glumly as he lurked behind a sculpture. *They were being more ruthless than ever.*

He took a moment out from his predicament to gaze around him. It was a large space, and high-value artwork dotted the room. There were huge, life-size dummies of the Ku Klux Klan by the Chatman brothers, alongside Stacey Lenins and Hursts. This was a big show.

Suddenly he caught site of Bonnie McCarten across the room, wearing a long black trench coat. She, too, looked nervous and was lurking among a group of art school hipsters.

He watched on with hatred as she tried to blend in with them. The art-schoolers were trying to close off their group but Bonnie would always walk around them to find another opening. They would then stroke their beards with unease and catch one another's' eye.

'HELP!' he saw one mouth to another, as Bonnie aligned her bulky body next to his. She looked up at another member of the group and began to nod along to what he was saying as gallery staff circled.

Reverend George quickly snuck over to a Ku Klux Klan figure and hid behind it. This put an extra two or three metres between Bonnie and himself.

He saw a group of liggers who had survived the purge hovering by a door, and realised that this was where the supply of food was coming from.

How obvious did they want to be? He would stay safely on his side of the room, he decided, minding his own business.

A tray emerged and the liggers flew at the waitress carrying it, causing her to disappear completely from sight.

Bonnie suddenly stormed up to the group. "Out of my way!" she shouted. "Out of my way!"

Reverend George watched, dumbfounded, as Bonnie shoved Deborah aggressively into the wall and grabbed a fist full of tiny sandwiches. They oozed through her fingers as she crunched them shut, and her other hand advanced towards the tray.

"Right, that's it. Get out!" screamed a woman in a red dress appearing from behind the chaos. She was red faced and her expression was one of deep disgust.

"Oh My God, that's Julia, the Director!" Reverend George heard a voice cry out. "She's like, on the Power 100 list."

"Just leave. Immediately." she spoke directly to Bonnie, who was depositing the sandwiches straight into her bag.

Bonnie withdrew her hand and pointed across the room at Reverend George who was still cowering behind the Ku Klux Klan. "I'm with him!" she squawked, cheese and smoked salmon flew off her finger tip. "He's a priest!"

Reverend George's blood - already simmering - now bubbled uncontrollably. His worst nightmare had just come true.

"No, you're not!" he roared, emerging from behind the robed dummy. "I can't stand her!"

"Oh, but you know her?" challenged the Director.

"Only because she keeps forcing herself on me," shrieked Reverend George, despairingly. His face was bright scarlet and every vein in his neck was now visible and throbbing above his dog-collar.

"LIAR!" screamed Bonnie.

"YOU'RE THE DEVIL!" Reverend George yelled back. He crossed his fingers and held them out towards Bonnie, as though to ward off the evil one.

He could hear a mixture of gasps and cackles around them but he did not care any longer. She had pushed him totally over the edge. Gallery staff surrounded the aggravated pair and gradually began to home in on Bonnie. A waiter extended an arm towards her unsurely but Bonnie backed away.

A more confident intern approached, and sensing this was her moment to shine, said assertively "Madam, can we talk about this outside?"

Bonnie backed into a corner, visibly out of breath. Her trench coat had become unbuttoned during the feeding frenzy and her eyes were wild.

"Like a crazed beast," someone whispered.

Suddenly Bonnie sprang into action. She dodged her oppressors and ran towards the other side of the gallery.

Staff gasped and then they too gradually broke into a jog as they followed her from one side of the gallery and then to another. Shocked guests then watched as this escalated into a full-on chase. Reverend George ran with the staff, cursing Bonnie between laboured breaths.

Drinks went flying and guests stumbled into art work. There was a chorus of screams as a Ku Klux Klan dummy wobbled and then plummeted sideways. On its way, it fell into another, and the whole collection toppled over like giant dominos.

As chaos took hold of the gallery, the liggers topped themselves up generously at abandoned drinks tables.

"THAT IS IT!" Screamed 'Power 100 Julia', clutching a bottle of champagne and mounting the front desk. Her hair was disheveled and damp with sweat as she pointed her finger around the entire gathering: "I WANT EVERYBODY IN THE GALLERY TO GET OUT NOW!"

Dom Dicker

Back in 1994 Dom Dicker dated a business woman, Sally Smith, who was big in interior design. He was slightly trimmer back then, and she had found his black beard and thick eyebrows 'sexy and dangerous'.

Dom played on this for a couple of years, donning dark sunglasses and brooding moodily at her side during various launches and functions. She, an aging Sloane, would dress him in biker boots and blazers from the Kings Road, his shoulder-length black hair would be tied back in a little ponytail, his shirts unbuttoned just enough to reveal the tip of a thick rug of chest hair that lay beneath. And Sally would complement his look, dressed in fringed leathers and expensive cowboy boots. *What a fashionable couple they were,* she would think smugly as they stood side by side drinking champagne.

Often he would rest one proprietorial hand on her backside, which was usually clad in tight white denim, and hold it there for hours as though it were stuck with the strongest adhesive. She would continue to hold intelligent conversations with guests, apparently unfazed by her boyfriend's rather unnatural pose. *Everyone was secretly turned on,* she would muse. *Probably all dying to swing with them.*

***

After a couple of years, Freeze happened and everybody in the business was obsessed with cashing in on the YBAs. Dom encouraged Sally to buy a gallery in Brick Lane. It was the perfect location - very cool and a hot-bed for up and coming artists. Sally swiftly acquiesced and a 'shell' was acquired.

"I like it!" exclaimed Sally as they queued for a bagel and watched an artistic looking man carry a couple of paint-spattered tyres across the street. "It's really vibey!"

"Yes - exactly as I said," Dom sighed tersely, irritated by the lack of recognition for his initiative.

"I know baby, that's why I bought it," said Sally, reassuringly.

Dom changed tack. He stepped in closer, pelvis first, and placed his hands on Sally's hips. "So… ," he said, smiling down at her through his big black beard. "What do you think we should call this little enterprise?"

"Well… as it's our project, I thought we could call it 'Smith and Dicker'," smiled Sally, excitedly.

Dom was silent. "We… could," he said slowly. "But don't you think that's a bit wordy?"

Sally flinched. "Well, what did you have in mind darling?"

"Umm, I thought just one of our names would be better…"

***

The Dom Dicker Gallery opened in summer 1998, and with the help of Sally's contacts, namely the house of Smaatchi, they were able to not only show the work of some big names but also gain corporate sponsorship. Early on, they showed a piece from the infamous Stacey Lenin's 'Stains of my Inner Soul' collection - a controversial clothes horse draped with dirty laundry. A tobacco company had sponsored them and they were given unlimited cigarettes - handing them out to the exclusive gathering of artists and collectors during the Private View. Unfortunately, the gallery became filled with so much smoke that one could not see the piece through the dark grey smog. Lenin's agent had been livid, and called Sally when the run was over to claim compensation as the returned artwork allegedly stank.

'Probably smells better than it did before!' barked Sally as she slammed down the phone.

However, these were the least of the gallery's problems. Dom spent every penny of their sales on 'business' jollies abroad and mountains of cocaine... as he snorted it one evening off their intern's naked stomach, Sally came by for a surprise visit. He looked on with horror, shirtless and hairy like a beast, as Sally snatched his keys from the desk and the Dom Dicker Gallery, toxic from debt, closed its doors that very night.

Despite this rather devastating loss, Dom had still managed to earn a bit of a name for himself in the art world. He morphed into a self-styled collector and continued to wear his shades and attend gallery openings in capital cities, mixing with the elite. Every time he walked through the doors of an invite-only event he marveled at how far he had come. How successful he was. He, Dom Dicker was part of the internationally renowned YBA movement.

***

In 2009, Dom began to notice a shift in the art scene. New faces were appearing at Private Views and he had absolutely no idea who these people were. In fact, he was not alone, nobody had a clue. Soon they were no longer strangers, they were *familiar*. They were at every major art show. These peoples' presence began to niggle Dom. There was always a middle-aged man in a baseball cap who seemed to be some kind of leader and was usually accompanied by a posse of scruffy nobodies.

One night, Dom could contain his curiosity no longer and deliberately loitered near these people in order to eavesdrop their conversation; now he learnt, to his horror, that the man in the cap worked at the Job Centre. They were just normal people! And yet here they were, at all the top private views!

Soon after, Dom casually mentioned to one of his acquaintances, the Director of Sproot McGowan Gallery, that the crowd in the corner were of no relevance to the art scene. "They aren't associated with the industry in any way, you know?" said Dom.

"Well, I imagine they must have been on the guest list," replied the Director wearily.

"But they're just drinking all your alcohol, I doubt they're going to buy any art," whispered Dom desperately.

"Ah yes, that reminds me, are you ever going to buy any art?" asked the Director.

Dom fell silent and looked down at his champagne; his acquaintance turned to talk to someone else.

As Dom stood there, miserably, a taxi pulled up outside. Dom immediately recognised the unmistakable 'Face of British Art' in the backseat. He watched as Stacey Lenin handed some money between the front seats to the driver and he hastily exited the gallery. In a flash he was at the taxi's back door, tugging it open in a rush of manic chivalry. A pink velvet shoe stepped out onto the pavement, its heel a gold hexagonal block. Stacey peered outside, cautiously.

"Hello Stacey!" purred Dom, leaning in. His voice had deepened a couple of octaves, and his right eyebrow shot up into a thick, furry hook.

Stacey stepped out of the cab. "Who are you?" she asked, nonchalantly, tightening the belt of her transparent plastic mac.

"You don't recognize me?" sighed Dom, tapping her arm playfully.

"No."

"I'm Dom Dicker, but people in the art world call me Dicky. Only special people, mind."

"Oh yeah, Dick-y. You're the one who fucked up my clothes horse, aren't you?"

"A memory that haunts me to this day," whined Dom, placing his hand on his heart and closing his eyes. "It was my ex-business partner's genius idea to hand out cigarettes that night... ," he finished through gritted teeth, so as to portray utter torment.

Stacey and Dom walked a few paces to the gallery together, and upon entry, Stacey was snatched from his side by sycophants. However, he took a back seat taking comfort in the knowledge that everybody would have seen their interaction outside and would know that Dom Dicker was still very much in business.

***

It was the summer of 2014, when Dom finally blew his top at the liggers.

He had just returned from Art Basal in Switzerland where he had found it almost impossible to rub shoulders with anybody important for the tsunami of scroungers that crashed through the parties.

As he browsed a water colour show in Bond Street he overheard, Mac the Australian, boast about his Swiss exploits.

"You would not believe it! We got into all the Press parties, and some of the VIP parties that the press weren't even invited to. We went to a brunch at Peggy Gerstein's, and had a private tour of her collection."

Mac's eyes glazed over as the memories took him into a euphoric trance.

Dom stormed over: "Oh, so it's YOU who's bringing all the liggers to Switzerland!" he declared so loudly that surrounding groups could hear.

Mac snapped out of his trance. "Huh?" he replied, in bewilderment.

"Back in the day, I would cruise around the lake in a speed boat with Jaz Joppling, but now I doubt he even bothers to go to the opening week thanks to all you vultures."

"Well actually, we saw him at the Marco Kwince opening party," Mac replied, politely. "I said hello, I was about to ask him what he thought of the show but then Moira cut her foot open on a broken glass..."

Audrey, the grey-haired ligger, let out a high pitched giggle. "Oh my God, do you remember? She had to lie on her back in the middle of the party with her foot in the air!"

Dom's mood turned darker with further disgust. "*What a disgrace.*"

"It was *sooo* nice to go to parties and not be thrown out," sighed Audrey. "We've had a terrible time with the *Winos* list."

"*Winos* list?" said Dom, his mood picking up.

"Yes, it's a list all the galleries have in Cork Street. It's called 'The Liggers of Cork Street'. They've got all our names and photos on it," Audrey said before adding. "So, you haven't been asked to leave any shows yet?"

"What? Why would I? I'm not a wino sweetheart," Dom sneered, "I'm a collector." He turned on his heel, and strode angrily away from the depraved congregation. As if he was one of them? She was really kooky that one, and not in a good way. Mad as a hatter.

He pretended to look at a painting as he glanced sideways, scouring the room for some more acceptable company. Dammit, he could still hear the liggers rabbiting on.

"He really doesn't know, does he?" Audrey was saying in a hushed voice.

"Well, don't tell him, just let him carry on believing he's a big cheese. It's better for everybody," said Mac. "Struth, that guy's got a nerve!"

Dom felt his face burn. *It couldn't be. No, surely not.* He, Dom Dicker, on *The List*? He was part of the YBA scene, everybody knew that. If he had been mistaken for a ligger, it would be the error of some silly intern. They were nearly as bad as liggers as far as he was concerned - not even worth the travel expenses. However much he reassured himself, Dom was becoming increasingly agitated. Damn these fuckwits getting under his skin like this. He would go back and challenge them, he decided. Why should he tolerate such hearsay?

As he made his way, a tall lady with blonde hair approached the group. Dom had noticed her upon arrival at the front desk. He had tried to catch her eye to give her a cheeky wink, but she had been too distracted by another guest. She wore a simple black dress and stilettos, and minimal jewellery. She was certainly no artist, and was thus surely some kind of employee. She had in her hand a piece of paper, and wore on her face a stern expression.

The List.

He watched her interrogate Mac.

Mac hooted with laughter, as though there had been a hilarious mistake. "Look, I've just flown in from Art Basal," he protested, reaching into his pocket and retrieving his wallet.

Dom watched as Mac pulled out what appeared to be a press pass and handed it to the lady. *'It has to be fake, or stolen,'* he seethed. She would see through it, and soon the whole bunch of liggers would be turfed out. Thank God somebody was finally clamping down on these jokers. This gallery was pro-actively separating the wheat from the chaff - just as he had advised the director of Sproof McGowan to do. He would no doubt be eating his hat right now, wishing he had nipped this nonsense in the bud.

The lady handed back the card to Mac: "Apologies, there's been a mistake, I think," she smiled.

"No worries!" boomed Mac, cheerfully. "This is a beautiful Sauvignon Blanc, by the way!"

The lady laughed. "A true Aussie!" she responded, hospitably.

Dom continued to watch her as she looked back down at The List and then scanned the room; he was mortified to find her gaze now halting upon himself. He watched, stunned, as all embers of warmth faded from her expression and the hostile stare retuned.

It had suddenly dawned on Dom what was about to happen. After all these years of networking, not to mention his important contribution to a scene that had changed art forever, he was to be turfed out of an opening like a peasant. He could not let it happen. He would not let it happen. IT WOULD NOT HAPPEN.

The lady now stood before him, lips pursed, the interrogation was about to begin... Dom closed his eyes, took a deep breath and nodded towards Mac, who had returned to his reminiscing. "I'm with him," he hissed.

Eustacia, Richard and Baddie

Eustacia wore big dark sunglasses, and stood propped up against a wall in the corner of the gallery. She was a very pretty woman and looked good for her 39 years. She did however bear the marks of malnourishment - rough skin and thin greasy brown hair, which was pulled back into a clip and fastened to the top of her head.

Through her dark lenses she could see a grand piano in the centre of the space, upon which a fellow ligger was plonking away vigorously.

As the keys were struck pink lights flashed in an umbrella shaped structure above the instrument. It appeared that each light was attached to a separate key with wires that rose up from beneath the mahogany encasement. She pulled her glasses down to her nose - the bulbs lit up in a pink shower as their corresponding key was struck. It was like a firework.

Eustacia felt happy for a moment, watching the artwork in a sedated trance. It was all rather lovely, although she wished that he could play something that didn't sound so clunky and tuneless.

Eustacia didn't know the man on the piano too well but she recognised his frizzy orange hair. She had seen him hanging around with Mac and Simon and had a very faint recollection that he was one of Simon's exes. They had all crashed a Carluccio's launch last week, if her memory served her correctly. Yet, in Eustacia's world last week could have been a month or five ago... it was all a drunken blur.

Her Anglo-Indian boyfriend, 'Baddie', appeared by the frizzy-haired ligger's side, and began to sing loudly. "SOMEONE LEFT THE CAKE OUT IN THE RAIN..."

Eustacia downed her wine, reached inside her leather shoulder bag and got a solid grip on her vodka bottle. She turned her back to the piano, and faced the corner, pouring the vodka into her wine glass. She had filled it half way when she felt a tap on her shoulder.

"Excuse me, please, but I'd like you to leave. You are not even drinking our beverages, let alone looking at our art," Eustacia turned to find she was being addressed by a slim woman in a black suit with a sleek dark bob and bright red lipstick.

"I was watching the piano... ," murmured Eustacia, pointing ahead. Her finger slowly veered off in the wrong direction.

"I think you're intoxicated. I'd like you to get your husband and leave."

"He's not my husband... ," replied Eustacia.

"Please, your presence is not required here," finished the gallerist, turning on her heel and making her way over to Baddie who was now waving his hands in the air as he bellowed.

"AND I'LL NEVER GET THAT RECIPE AGAIN... OH NO!"

***

Eustacia, Baddie and the frizzy-haired piano player staggered down the road.

"It was all because of you two!" cried Eustacia. "Baddie, you were singing, and you, what's your name?"

"Richard," said Baddie.

"Well, Richard, when you played that piano, it sounded awful."

"Well, it was supposed to sound awful," said Richard, striding ahead. "That was the whole point presumably, the keys were all in the wrong position. It had been re-strung."

"Yeah right, don't make out like it's the art. You just can't play piano," shouted Eustacia. "Anyway, where are we going to go now?"

"There's some kind of Astro-Physics convention at the Commonwealth Club," said Richard. His voice was extremely posh and high pitched. "I'm absolutely famished, I bet they've got some canapés."

"Do we look like fucking scientists?" slurred Eustacia wrapping a green scarf around her head, her sunglasses glinting in the street lamps. Baddie hiccupped next to her.

"No," said Richard. "But perhaps if you just don't speak... Let's take my Rolls." He nodded towards a vintage style Rolls Royce glinting in the dark.

"Woooooow!" cried Eustacia.

"You have a Rolls Royce! Mate, what you doing crashing physics conventions with us?" Baddie gaped.

"It's basically an exquisite antique on wheels," said Richard ignoring the question.

They piled enthusiastically into the car, Eustacia in the front and Baddie in the back.

"Things are looking up!" said Eustacia. "Just make sure you drive around the front of the convention a few times with the windows down so that they can all see us."

"I took this car once and drove it to Versailles," said Richard, as they cruised along. "I sped through the gates and pulled up right in front of the palace, and had my picture taken."

"What? You can't be allowed cars at the entrance of Versailles!" cried Eustacia.

"No. I had about thirty seconds before Security rushed out. Just enough time to get out and sit on the bonnet for a picture without them in the background."

"Who took the picture?"

"Oh, one of my mother's servants, he came with me that day. I said 'I'll take you to Paris if you take a photo of me outside Versailles in my Rolls'. We drove straight there from London, and straight back after."

Eustacia and Baddie were silent.

"I had the photo made into coasters, they're all at my house in Holland Park."

"You live in Holland Park? Seriously mate, you don't need to be blagging your way into conventions," said Baddie incredulously from the back.

"I like to save my money," Richard replied. "So... Eustacia... ?"

"Yeah?"

"Your name?"

"It's from a Thomas Hardy novel."

"Oh, I see. Eustacia Vye."

"Yes. Eustacia Vye."

"Return of the Native."

"Something like that."

"Eustacia Vye was a very tragic woman."

Baddie howled with laughter and pointed at the back of his girlfriend. "So's she!"

Eustacia drew a stick man in the condensation on the window and watched as the water fragmented the image and trickled down the pane. "I'm pretty tragic, yes, thank you Baddie."

***

Richard, Eustacia and Baddie approached the Commonwealth club. They had parked the car behind the building and walked around to the front.

As they neared the door Richard suddenly hunched over and crept up behind a pair of gentlemen dressed in formal attire. The gentlemen wore plastic badges on their overcoats and were deep in discussion.

Eustacia and Baddie held back and shared a cigarette as Richard lurked behind the two men, still as a predator. Oblivious to their stalker, the men continued with their discussion, whilst a frizz of hair loomed behind them. After a couple of minutes, the men nodded at each other and turned and strolled back inside the building.

Eustacia and Baddie walked over to Richard who still remained in his predatory position.

"I think it's a conference regarding Space Elevators," whispered Richard.

"What the hell are Space Elevators?" cried Eustacia.

"What they say on the box. Come on," said Richard scampering up the stairs.

They walked through the grand arched entrance, and found themselves surrounded by bronze statues of scholars and politicians. A beautiful marble staircase stood before them, curving elegantly to the side. The three intruders moved towards it.

"Can I help you?" an elderly bespectacled gentleman stood behind them. He was dressed very smartly in a blue velvet waistcoat, and a red cravat. His hair was snow white and combed to the side.

Richard bowed deeply before him, and Eustacia and Baddie exchanged unsure glances.

"We have come for the Space Elevator convention."

"Do you mean the Freemen's sit down dinner?" replied the man, his eyes darting suspiciously around the three.

"Oooh, sit down dinner! Why, yes Sir," chirped Richard.

"Well the hors d'oeuvres have already been served. And in addition, everybody who was invited is in attendance - the table is quite full. There must be some kind of misunderstanding."

"Well, of course. A misunderstanding," said Richard, lifting a finger in the air with enlightenment. "Now please don't feel foolish, just shove us on the end."

The old man laughed as though trying to suppress his outrage. "I meant a misunderstanding on your behalf. Now, please excuse me."

He walked past them and took hold of the banister of the marble staircase; Richard, Eustacia and Baddie watched on as he ascended.

The man turned around. "There is security in operation upstairs," he warned before continuing on his way.

"Come on mate, I'm Indian, I'm a scientist!" shouted Baddie desperately. But he did not turn again.

Eustacia let out a huge sigh and staggered towards the archway. She could hear Richard muttering to Baddie. "It's because of her breath, it smells like a distillery!"

Eustacia couldn't be bothered to reply, she was too busy rummaging around in her bag for her vodka and thinking about their next jaunt.

"Maybe we can just drive around and look for something," she slurred, as they found themselves back on the pavement.

"Hold on, if there's a dinner upstairs, then I want to know where the kitchen is," said Richard angrily.

"Come on, mate," said Baddie. "Even we wouldn't do that."

But Richard crouched on the pavement and sniffed, his nostrils flared like a wild animal.

"Shit, he's fucking crazy!" screamed Eustacia, laughing.

Richard appeared to catch a scent and crept along the ground. Suddenly he stood up and bounded around the corner, Baddie and Eustacia scurried behind in pursuit.

Eventually they caught up with him and found themselves back near the spot where they had parked the car. They stopped dead in their tracks when they saw that Richard had mounted a spiked gate that barricaded a metal stairway to the basement. His eyes were fixated on something down below.

Eustacia peered over the railing and could see that a fire door was slightly ajar and the unmistakable clanging of pots and pans could be heard echoing from within.

"Come on Richard," said Baddie. "This is way out there now."

Richard put a finger to his lips. "Shhh."

He slithered over the other side of the gate, and dropped onto the stairs. A shrill alarm sounded.

"Oh fuck!" cried Eustacia half giggling, half panicking. "Back up Richard, quick!"

But Richard was no longer in earshot. He was down the stairs and through the Fire Door.

"Oh mate! Oh my God," shouted Baddie, grabbing Eustacia's vodka. "He's gunna get done. We're gunna get done!"

Within twenty seconds Richard emerged from the kitchen and raced up the stairs with a large object in one of his hands. As he ascended Eustacia realised with disbelief that it was a frying pan. Shouting could be heard from below and a shocked cook appeared in the doorway.

"What are you doing?" the cook shouted to Richard.

Richard appeared to be in a panic now. He scrambled up the gate with the frying pan still clamped firmly in his hand. Spaghetti fell to the ground in clumps. A group of kitchen workers had gathered below, gaping at this very unusual burglary.

Richard dropped to the ground and panting, he fumbled in his pocket for his keys. Eustacia saw with horror that three or four people had now appeared from around the corner of the building and were rushing towards them. One figure shone a light in their faces. It must be Security.

Richard retrieved his keys and rushed towards the back of the car. He threw the boot open and placed the frying pan and what was left of its contents carefully inside.

Eustacia and Baddie watched on in stunned silence, as Richard slammed the book shut and jumped into the driver's seat.

"Hey!" screamed Eustacia as the engine started.

Baddie and Eustacia rushed to the passenger side but Richard reversed. They pounded at the windows but Richard was not stopping for anyone. The car screeched off, leaving them on the kerb with a band of guards and cooks approaching.

"Oh, you fucking mad prick!" screamed Baddie as the Rolls disappeared down the street.

"Run!" yelped Eustacia, and the couple lumbered off as fast as their alcohol-saturated bodies would take them. As they turned the corner their eyes fell upon a row of dustbins, and they dived behind them breathlessly, clinging to each other as thundering feet ran past. Two minutes later, they heard panting voices.

"He must have picked them up," came a booming Northern voice.

"What on earth happened?" said another.

"He just came in and started looking around the kitchen. At first I thought he was some kind of employee."

"Well, I know my spaghetti's good and everything..."

Laughter could be heard and they appeared to retreat.

"Baddie, this is really fucking embarrassing," said Eustacia as they crawled out from behind the bins.

"Woman, this is next level shit!" cried Baddie, dusting himself off.

Baddie and Eustacia swigged the remainder of their vodka and walked some miles down the quiet, residential back streets of West London. Suddenly they saw the flash of a white dress some yards ahead, and they stopped in their tracks.

"Did you see that Eustacia?" gasped Baddie.

They paused, and then they saw a white car too, and a series of camera flashes.

"A wedding!" shrieked Eustacia excitedly.

"This is it!" shouted Baddie. "This is our reward for everything we've been through tonight!" He punched the air.

"I love you Baddie!" sighed Eustacia, leaning into her beau.

Baddie slung his arm around her, as they made their way towards the bright lights ahead. Romantic songs began to dance in the air.

"Me and you are like that film by Tarantino... but wino versions... " he mused.

"We're Natural Born Liggers," smiled Eustacia blissfully.

Meryl

"Oh Christ my ankle!" shrieked Meryl as she wobbled in mid-air, clinging on to Ashpak's trouser leg. She cranked her neck back and looked to the side, catching a glimpse of the dark green canal swirling below.

"Pull her up, Ashpak!" James John wheezed from the ground. His voice was muffled by the straps of Meryl's sandals which were clamped in his mouth, while the rest of the shoes dangled below his chin. Both his hands were stretched up, each holding one of Meryl's feet.

"I can't!" exclaimed their accomplice Ashpak. He had straddled the wall above them but had not managed to locate a secure enough notch on the other side to enable a safe descent. "There's nothing!" He despaired, exploring the wall with his free leg while Meryl hugged the other.

"Come on!"

"How?"

"Eeeeuuuuugh!"

The sound of motor boats and water taxis could be heard whirring in the distance, out in the Venetian waters. But no boats would come up this exclusive stretch, it was the mouth to the Giardini, where the greatest art exhibition in all the world took place - the Venice Biennale. It was restricted water, a passage solely for those attending the Red Lion Awards, and the event inside would be well underway.

As the liggers grappled at the wall, Meryl wailed in pain. Her arthritis wasn't up to this. Somewhere in the back of her mind she was aware of one of the engines becoming a little louder.

"I can't take it any longer!" moaned James, his arms trembled with the load and they slowly began to part taking Meryl's feet with them.

"No!" she screamed, as she felt her skirt rip.

A balmy breeze now blew through a hole in the strained behind of the garment as she froze, spread-eagled.

The engine had become louder and all three liggers turned their heads. A black speedboat glistened in the sunset, and as Meryl squinted, she could just about make out two humungous armed guards standing aboard.

A smaller silhouette stood serenely in the middle.

"Just think of the champagne, just think of the champagne," she heard James mutter from below.

"Oh shut up!" she hissed. She was the one who was seventy years of age - James was at least a decade younger. The three interlopers froze.

The boat, now just a stone's throw away, cruised at a painfully slow pace as it neared the contorted triumvirate that hung over the Giardini walls.

Now Meryl had a chance to get a good look at the people who stood on board. The guards wore navy uniforms and had matching black goatees. It was as if they were twins. Meryl suddenly noticed a colossal machine gun resting across one of the men's arms, and she swallowed a scream.

Her eyes now darted to the figure in the middle - a petite woman in a pilot's hat. The woman moved the pilot's cap ever so slightly up so that she could look ahead, and as she did so Meryl nearly fell backwards. It was Koko Ono!

By some miracle Koko Ono and her guards had failed to notice them and Meryl felt relief wash over her as they began to slowly float past.

Then to Meryl's utmost horror, the engine cut out completely, and silence hung heavily in the air broken only by the lazy lapping of the canal and the sudden tweet of a bird. A disembodied crackly voice emerged from one of the guard's earpiece.

"They are asking for a few more minutes Signora Ono, before you make your grand entrance," he informed her, in a deep growling Italian voice.

Meryl reasoned that she now had no choice but to fall into a meditative trance. She prayed Ashpak and James would somehow do the same, otherwise the only place they would be going tonight was in the canal - or a body bag judging by the look of those oafs.

Mind over body. Mind over body thought Meryl, frantically remembering her Pilates sessions some years ago. *The body is merely a vessel. A strong powerful vessel.*

Five unbearable minutes later the engine restarted and the boat zoomed off.

"I've got it!" cried Ashpak triumphantly. "I've found a notch." Now he was able to haul a traumatised Meryl up to the top of the wall, her legs frozen akimbo as she ascended. *Like rigor mortis or something,* she thought miserably.

Once on the other side, the three liggers collapsed in a wheezing heap. Meryl rummaged in her evening bag for a comb and ran it through her dyed auburn hair, as she fought to catch her breath. She pulled out a pearly compact mirror that her mother had given her and opened it, whilst rummaging for her lipstick. She pursed her lips to apply a magenta, which she did with two quick strokes. When she unpursed her lips she was displeased to see the pink goop now stuck in folds around her mouth. She removed it with a tissue and a bit of spit, and reapplied with careful dabs.

She turned to James. "Please tell me you brought my shoes over?"

"I tried to throw them over but I think they got stuck in the tree."

***

The party was in full swing and as they neared; they could see a pair of young European women drinking champagne. One of the women wore a sheer hooded dress and high heeled shoes that were made to look like pineapples. The heel and straps were made of brown and yellow spiky leather, and from the ankle green leaf shapes shot up in all directions.

The lady with pineapple shoes had an 'Industry' badge clipped to her dress, and her companion, dressed in more conservative attire wore a 'Press' badge.

"So, what are we?" asked Ashpak, pulling a leaf out of his hair.

"Three nobodies looking to party," said James.

"Sounds good to me!" said Meryl, turning to laugh at James. She had regained some kind of poise and her hair now sparkled copper in the sunset.

Ashpak laughed too. "Yes, but if they ask, are we 'Industry' or 'Press'?"

"Er, press, I think," said James.

"Press it is!" said Meryl decisively, with a deep nod to the side.

Suddenly Ashpak dropped to one knee and Meryl and James stood back, wondering what was going on.

Ashpak whipped a camera from his pocket and proceeded to take a series of pictures, letting off several blinding flashes. The lady in the pineapple shoes stopped and smiled, she placed one hand on her hip. Meryl observed the journalist next to her sticking out her jaw bone to avoid a double chin as she too smiled for

Ashpak.

A pair of security guards strolled by and as they passed Ashpak popped up onto his feet again.

"Ahhh, I like your style!" said Meryl. "Now, let's get some well-deserved champagne."

***

The liggers had partied for about half an hour in the Giardini. The champagne flowed freely; in fact they had been handed their own bottle in a bucket when they reached the bar and they were not alone. Nearly everybody stood clasping their own bucket as they mingled with the sparkling throng.

Meryl, James and Ashpak watched as a parade of giant tattooed burlesque dancers circled the party in Venetian masks, their bulky inked flesh oozed over PVC corsets and wobbled in the dusk as they danced for the VIP guests. It was some kind of performance art, courtesy of the Finnish Pavilion.

"What a night!" toasted James, lifting his glass.

"Fabulous!" breathed Meryl. "Just fabulous."

Suddenly a weedy masked individual appeared before Ashpak, Meryl and James. His mask was one of the more macabre designs, a smooth black texture with a long decorative beak. They looked on at him expectantly. Did he want to converse with them?

Suddenly Meryl was overwhelmed by a sense of familiarity. She squinted and looked a little closer. She recognised those two beady eyes that glinted out from behind the mask. Who was this mystery guest?

In a flash he was gone.

"Who on Earth was that?" cried Ashpak.

"I'm sure we know him Ashpak," Meryl sighed.

"Me too!" exclaimed James. "I could just sense we knew that bloke."

"Well, maybe in a past life!" Meryl said shrugging her shoulders. "Anyway, I'm desperate for a pee!"

"Oh, well hurry up, the ceremony's about to begin," urged Ashpak, whose face bore a euphoric grin.

Meryl left James and Ashpak and stumbled around the corner. The Giardini occupied a vast terrain, with broad gravel paths leading to the forty huge pavilions, each hosting an exhibition from a different country.

"Excuse me, where are the toilets?" Meryl asked a man in a blazer.

"Oh, they're by the main pavilion," he replied.

"Ah!" said Meryl. If memory served her correctly, this building was all the way over by the official entrance. It was the big white building that was covered in hundreds of life-like pigeons where everybody always scratched their heads waiting for them to move.

"The one with the pigeons?" she confirmed.

"Yes."

"Thanks, but I think I'll have to find an alternative!" she replied.

The man gave her a polite smile and continued on his way. Meryl turned back to the party where she could see that the ceremony was now underway. Most heads now faced a small stage where a gentleman was talking into a microphone. There was a large backdrop to the stage, and everything behind it was obscured from the entire audience.

"Ah-ha!" said Meryl thinking out loud. A few heads turned and she staggered forth.

Once behind the stage her eyes fell upon a little bush. She scouted round quickly and ascertained it was not in anyone's line of vision. Meryl flew towards the shrubbery, she could barely hold it in a minute longer. It was now dark, and she was quite confident she would not be disturbed here.

***

Koko Ono took to the stage, dressed in her trademark tailored suit with flared trousers. She was greeted by thunderous applause. The ceremony had been delayed slightly, as a microphone had gone missing backstage and they had had to send a pissed intern down to the main pavilion to get another one.

Now she accepted her Golden Lion trophy - a glittering statue of the beast itself with her name engraved on a plaque beneath its feet.

KOKO ONO - LIFETIME ACHIEVEMENT AWARD

"What energy," she began, looking around at the gathering of artists, collectors and media. A warm applause and a few whoops greeted her words.

She held her lion into the air and leaned into the mic.

"Lions are beautiful mothers, and passionate lovers," she told the audience.

They applauded again.

"Yeah!" a man shouted out.

Koko smiled and opened her mouth to continue...

Suddenly a gushing sound could be heard. Koko turned her head confused and looked around. It was really loud, like someone had turned on a giant tap full blast.

The audience began to talk amongst themselves, debating where this peculiar sound was coming from. Was it part of the performance? Some kind of sound installation?

The gushing went on for a further two or three minutes while Koko stood awkwardly on the stage. Then there was a loud amplified crackle followed by a few deafening squeaks that sounded like feedback.

Koko looked to the wings for guidance but her assistant shrugged her shoulders helplessly.

Koko leaned towards the microphone and resumed: "The Biennale is always filled with such magic and mystery... ," she continued, recapturing the adoring gaze and attention of the crowd.

Meryl appeared from behind the stage, adjusting her skirt, and snuck into the first few rows of audience. She turned to face Koko and clapped along.

"In fact, I always think of Venice like the Island in the Tempest," Koko philosophised, making an extravagant gesture in the air.

Meryl cheered, and marveled at the evening's successes.

***

Ashpak and James were crumpled together in a hiccupping wreck on the church steps. It was midnight and they had missed the last boat back to the mainland.

"We'll have to get the sea taxi," shouted Meryl, pointing to the lone boat tied to the jetty.

"You heard him, it's one hundred euros," James complained.

"That defeats the whole purpose of us staying in the trailer park,' agreed Ashpak.

"It does… but look what I found," said Meryl mysteriously. She reached into her handbag and pulled out two little rectangular pieces of plastic. She staggered over to James and Ashpak and held them in front of their faces.

"Press passes! You got press passes?" cried Ashpak ecstatically.

"Uh huh, I found them on the floor," said Meryl smugly putting them back in her bag.

"This means we can go to the last day of press week tomorrow," shrieked James standing up and then immediately falling back down.

"Yep, apparently there's food and drink galore. But look, whoever they belong to will go to the Biennale and ask for new ones, so we need to get there very early before these ones are cancelled. Let's make sure we get a good night's sleep in our trailer tonight so we can make sure we're there first thing!"

The liggers bounded to the sea taxi, and sailed merrily along the dark canal. Beautiful old buildings were lit up from inside and they gazed at them in wonder. Suddenly they were out of the canals and into open water. Their path to Fusina, their mainland destination, was outlined by lamps used to guide oil tankers. The cool breeze blew through Meryl's hair and she felt a surge of empowerment - most women her age were holed up on their own, shivering in their slippers. But not Meryl. She was not past her sell by date, not by a long shot. She was queen of the scene. She had done 'normal', residing in Kent and working as an English teacher, but she would never look back. She had never felt more alive than since she had become a ligger.

As the boat pulled up at the Fusina camp site, Meryl, James and Ashpak took their time to count the money. They reluctantly handed over 33.33 Euros each and the mood lowered as they made their way up the gravel path.

"What a rip off!" grumbled James.

"There goes a week's groceries!" Meryl sighed.

They trudged through the dark campsite. Pop music could be heard across the expanse of tents, trailers and darkness, and a few shouts. It was the Australian Contiki Tour, a big group of travelling youngsters, sightseeing and partying across Europe. The group would station themselves in Fusina for a couple of evenings, and then a fresh batch would arrive, while the others trucked off.

"Sounds like one of those toga parties," said James his voice picking up. "It might be a different coach load tonight."

"Now, come on," said Meryl, dubiously. "I think we've had enough excitement for one night, I don't think we need to try and get in with that bloomin' Contiki tour again."

"Yeah, we've been partying with Koko Ono, thank you Contikis - put that in your pipe and smoke it," said Ashpak smugly. The teenage Aussies had not exactly welcomed the liggers with open arms the night before, when they had loitered hopefully near the rowdy congregation.

"Let's get some sleep. I think we're going to have a very busy day tomorrow," said Meryl wisely.

***

Meryl awoke around seven thirty. She gasped for air as the trailer baked in the morning sun. She looked to her left. On the other bed lay James, on his back, his pasty limbs splayed in every direction. On the floor, in the aisle between their two beds snoozed Ashpak, letting out little rippling snores with every breath.

Meryl groped the shelf next to her and felt for her sunglasses. They were jet black with diamante studs. She placed them over her eyes and felt a little relief from the pounding sensation in her head.

She was just about to nod off again when she remembered.

"The press passes!" she shouted as she sat up bolt upright. The sunglasses fell down her nose. Ashpak and James stirred. Meryl grabbed her pillow and thumped Ashpak over the head with it.

"Owww!" he cried clutching his head and rocking.

James opened one eye and then groaned.

"Get up now!" squawked Meryl, thrashing round the trailer like a big mother hen. She grabbed her wash bag, threw on her bath robe and opened the trailer door. A cool breeze greeted her.

"Oh wow!" cried Ashpak as it blew through the trailer.

"Woooow!" echoed James, resting his arms behind his head. The breeze fanned his grey armpit hair and he sighed blissfully.

Meryl slammed the door shut - she had seen quite enough of that. She descended the three steps onto the grass and strode out along the path.

An oil tanker cruised alongside her as she made her way to the bathroom, and let out a big honk.

'That'll wake them up,' she laughed to herself.

On her way to the bathrooms, Meryl stopped off at the campsite shop to buy some water. As she peered dimly about the shop in her sunglasses, a newspaper headline caught her eye: 'Entire Sicilian Mafia Gang Wiped Out By Rivals'.

She craned her neck forward and lifted up her sunglasses, grimacing at the brightness. She was quite sure she recognized the man in the accompanying picture.

"Barbieri... Barbieri," she muttered, squinting at the caption. She knew this name but her hangover was too intense to solve the puzzle and she wandered to the till, defeated.

As she fished in her handbag for change, her hands brushed against the coveted press passes.

Today was going to be a good day - she could feel it!

***

With the aid of proprietary analgesics and sheer will-power, Ashpak, Meryl and James had managed to catch the eight o'clock boat to Piazza San Marco. They sat on the top deck and had been absolutely delighted when their friend, 'Matthew of Mayfair' had unexpectedly joined them aboard.

Matthew had managed to get a last minute flight and had arrived at Fusina late last night. Matthew lived in a council flat in Mayfair and always wore his own hand-painted shirts and trousers, decorated with colourful brush strokes.

The liggers spent most of the journey problem-solving. How could two press passes get four of them in? After a lot of debate - which had brought their headaches crashing back - Meryl cleared her throat.

"If myself and James go in, we can wait ten minutes and then James can come out bringing both the press passes," she said in tones of great seriousness. "This will allow him and one other person back in. Now, once three of us are in, I can then come out ten minutes later with both the press passes and collect the remaining person."

Everybody sat in silence whilst they considered this plan.

"Everybody clear?" asked Meryl.

"Yes, but that's what I said half an hour ago," grumbled Ashpak.

"No you didn't!" exploded Meryl. "You wanted me and James to scale the walls again, and you and Matthew to use the press passes. Even though I found them!"

The liggers sat in silence as they cruised into Venice. They passed beautiful grand buildings with gilded stucco and pastel colourings. Pink glass lamps on silvery posts aligned the waters, and the sky was blue. The canal sparkled emerald today and the walkways were empty - the hour of the tourists was not yet upon them.

They docked outside the Doge's palace and walked the twenty minute stretch along to the Giardini, strolling under arches and over bridges. They chattered and giggled about the trip so far, and filled Matthew in on their great adventures last night.

Matthew hooted with laughter as they described their climb over the wall, and Ashpak demonstrated the armed guards by cradling an imaginary machine gun in his arms with a deathly expression.

"But the most incredible thing was when Meryl pissed over the top of Koko Ono's speech," cried James wiping tears of laughter from his eyes.

Meryl stopped dead in her tracks and the colour drained from her face.

"Huh?"

***

All four liggers had successfully entered the final day of the Venice Biennale press week, thanks to Meryl's plan. They had already explored several pavilions by ten o'clock and had been treated to an opera about a car crash in the Hungarian pavilion, a big pile of rubble in the Dutch pavilion and an army of 'Peace Soldiers' in the Korean Pavilion. Meryl liked the latter in particular, and had requested several photos with the muscular Korean performers: men dressed in flower-patterned combat gear. They had posed in front of a wall with matching flower-patterned wall paper, so that only their chiseled faces and bare, bulging biceps stood out amongst the camouflage.

Now, they rushed to the French pavilion where, rumour had it, a brunch was about to be served. On arrival, they saw to their delight tables full of mini-croissants and rows of champagne being poured. They gazed over longingly as they awaited the green light to dive in.

A beautiful black woman dressed in pink velvet shorts stood on the steps talking to a couple of business types.

"That's the artist!" Meryl heard somebody hiss.

After ten agonizing minutes, the lady looked down to the crowd. "Ladies and Gentlemen," she said brightly in a strong French accent. "We are delighted to welcome you to France's final brunch. So... Bon Appetit!"

The liggers ran to the tables. They grabbed napkins and filled them with croissants. They downed two or three glasses of champagne and then rested another three between their fingers, before carefully turning and making their way through the crowds of press who were waiting calmly behind them.

"Er, hungry?" asked one journalist.

"Oh, we're always hungry," chuckled James.

As they crammed their mouths and licked their fingers, they also took the opportunity to confer on the evening ahead.

"Any news on the parties yet?" asked Meryl, her moustache of croissant crumbs moving up and down as she chomped.

"No," sighed James. They could see Matthew, still standing by the drinks table. He was being circled by the world media and they were tapping him on the shoulder to take pictures of him in his colourful painted outfit.

"We don't need to try anymore!" said Ashpak brightly. "Matthew of Mayfair is here!"

***

It was six in the evening and the Iraqi party was about to kick off. They were in a courtyard somewhere and had spent a glorious day brunch-crawling in the sun. They had viewed more weird and wonderful art and were gearing up for the evening festivities.

They found themselves chatting to a young English girl with wavy blonde hair and a little upturned nose. She had come to the press week with a friend, they learned.

"So, you're not an artist or anything?" quizzed James.

"Oh God no," she laughed. "I like art but I'm a nurse."

"Ah well, I'm afraid the only thing we can nurse is a hangover!" said Ashpak, and the liggers all howled with laughter. The young girl laughed along too, before leaning in.

"My friend tells me there's a really good party tonight."

The liggers bent forward in unison and Meryl tucked her hair behind her ears so she could hear every word.

"Erm, wow okay, you guys really like to party!" she laughed. "Erm, anyway, it's on an island out in the lagoon."

"So how do we get there?" asked Meryl.

The girl lowered her voice slightly: "Well, apparently, you have to go down to the water at about eight o'clock, just by the Giardini, and a woman comes along holding a balloon. And that's the code. It's like, really exclusive."

Meryl felt James nudge her in the ribs, and she had to suppress a squeal of delight.

"We'll be there," said Ashpak loudly. Meryl could tell he was trying to keep his cool, but his eyes were crazed with excitement.

They had struck Venetian gold.

***

It was quarter to eight and Meryl, Ashpak, James and Matthew of Mayfair stood at the docks of the Giardini. They had spread out in front of the wall so that they could see round all the corners and an intensity hung in the air. They did not want to miss this.

By five to eight a small group had assembled and it had been communicated in hushed whispers that they were all waiting for the 'balloon lady'.

At five past eight, people began to sigh and look at their watches. The liggers, on the other hand, were in the early stages of a meltdown.

"What if this is all a lie, or a practical joke?" despaired James. "I mean, come on! A lady with a balloon? God, we're bloody fools, that's what we are. And now, we're out of the loop. That Iraqi party will be over so we won't be able to go back there now!"

"She seemed like a nice girl," replied Ashpak nervously.

"She's just a nurse!" shouted James. He kicked the wall and buried his face in his hands. "Christ!"

Suddenly, the sound of heels could be heard clip-clopping on the walkway and a tall olive-skinned lady emerged in a tight red dress, beaming from ear to ear. In her right hand she clasped a big bunch of blue, red and yellow balloons. She truly was a magnificent vision drenched in the golden sunset.

"Been waiting long?" she asked casually.

"Yes!" James whimpered. "Oh, thank God!"

"Are you a mirage or are you real?" whispered Ashpak.

The lady laughed, and beckoned with her finger.

The small party followed her round the corner to the water's edge where a smart white boat was waiting for them. It too was decorated with red, yellow and blue balloons and a waiter with a tray of cocktails stood on the deck.

Meryl wondered if she had died and gone to heaven.

A velvet rope was unclipped and the party hopped aboard, one by one. They had all settled down in the white leather interior when there was a shout.

"Hey, are you the balloon lady?"

The liggers looked out through the windows. It was the nurse!

"We were invited to the party," her companion - a tall man in his early twenties - explained.

The lady gasped. "Oh my goodness, there is only one space left on the boat!"

Without a moment's hesitation, the man leapt aboard. Meryl blinked.

"Sorry Flora, but it's work you know, I can't miss it," he shouted. "You can try the Icelandic Pavilion, I think they're having drinks there."

The liggers looked at each other.

"What a beast," muttered Matthew, looking out of the window at Flora, who could not conceal her hurt and disappointment. Meryl found herself in a deep moral dilemma. Could they really leave this poor girl on her own, when she had so kindly tipped them off? It was, after all, their fault that there was no room for her. She peered out at her, and wrestled with her conscience.

I'm old, she's young. She's got her whole life to go to parties Meryl reassured herself, settling back into her seat.

The engine started.

"Wait!"

The liggers gasped as Ashpak stood up and raced up the stairs onto the deck.

"You must go, my dear!" said Ashpak.

"Ashpak, no!" cried Meryl standing up and hitting her head on the roof of the boat.

"Yes Meryl," said Ashpak bravely. "This is the right thing to do."

Without further word he grabbed the bewildered nurse's hand and pulled her on board.

He turned to face the liggers and gave his friends one last heart-wrenching stare before he flung himself back onto the jetty.

The engine started and Meryl let out a sob. She pressed her face to the window as the boat bounced over the waves and into the lagoon.

Ashpak's sad lonely figure grew smaller and smaller but they were away in an inky green seascape - their destination unknown. Leafy little islands emerged and disappeared .

Every time an island grew larger Meryl wondered if their little boat was going to dock, but it sped dutifully past.

Flora the Nurse came and sat next to Meryl.

"Bless that Ashram!" she cried.

"Ashpak!" sniffed Meryl.

Flora was silent. "He's nicer than my friend," she said after a while.

The journey must have lasted a good twenty minutes before the boat finally slowed down.

"Oh wow!" shrieked Flora, pointing ahead.

Meryl squinted out of the window and could now see a small island. It was ablaze with a million candles.

As the boat pulled in, the liggers and the small party alighted. The boat and the balloon lady departed back to Venice. They said that they had another secret batch of guests to collect.

They followed a path lit up with tall, blazing torches, eventually reaching a spacious lawn where a giant marquee awaited.

Meryl, James and Matthew were overcome with silent awe.

They accepted a cocktail and then settled into a plump leather sofa inside the marquee.

"To Ashpak," said Meryl sombrely raising her glass.

"What a bloke," said James wistfully, shaking his head.

***

It was midnight and the party was in full swing. Meryl, James, Matthew of Mayfair and Flora the nurse had drained several bottles of champagne, danced all over the lawn and watched 'art clowns' blow fire into big heart-shaped flames. Meryl had been to many fabulous parties but this was quite possibly the best yet.

As she sank blissfully into the sofa, she was suddenly aware that she had company.

A handsome, rugged man was topping up her glass. She squinted through eyes, half blurred by alcohol, half by cataracts. He must have been about sixty.

"My name's Filippo, and I think you're absolutely gorgeous," he said, taking a seat next to her. He had an Italian accent.

Meryl hooted with laughter.

"Well, that's very kind of you Filippo but I think you must have had too much champagne."

"Oh I know what I like," Filippo purred. He wore a dark green shirt and faded black jeans. His hair was white and fell over his olive green eyes.

Yum thought Meryl. She fluttered her eyelashes. "What is it you like then Filippo?"

Filippo leaned in.

"I like my woman to be like my wine," he said with a heartfelt sincerity. "Complex and mature..."

Filippo and Meryl became locked in deep conversation. Filippo was from Milan and looked after the estate of the famous deceased artist Federico Beacon, she learnt.

Meryl gasped with outrage as he told her how angry relatives were now trying to seize this from his protection.

She touched his arm as he told her of the bitter legal battle he was entrenched in.

They gazed into one another's eyes.

"There's a fantastica gala in Chioggia," he suddenly announced. "Is a really swanky do - everyone who's anyone is going to be there. They're all heading out after the Biennale... ," he said.

Meryl leaned in breathlessly.

"...The only problem is, I don't have a date..." Filippo sighed.

Meryl knocked back her champagne and slapped him on the thigh.

"You do now!"

Fight for your Right...

September had come around, and the Cork Street Winos braced themselves for a period of austerity. In the golden age, this time of year had been one of great excitement; the galleries closed for the whole of August, and re-opened with fresh energy and enthusiasm, sometimes marking the new season with innovative and original art

This year however, a sadness hung in the air. Over the months, the galleries had made it clear that liggers would no longer be welcome, and all other possibilities for gate-crashing had now been exhausted.

Even though the liggers had gradually come to terms with this, many found it difficult to let go and would meet in groups at the corner of Albermarle Street at the foot of a big bronze statue of a horse. Here, they would gather at six on a Thursday evening to keep the spark alive.

"We're a bunch of saddos," said Deborah to Audrey and Moira as they strolled aimlessly around the area one day, having loitered at the horse for the past hour sharing a bottle of rosé.

"Well, I think we'd be sadder if we were at home, staying in obediently," said Audrey firmly. "We're all human beings. The only difference between us and them is that we don't have any money."

"I agree!" said Moira, pumping the air with her fist. "We have to stand up for our rights."

As they passed the Bill Brown gallery, they all turned their heads to gaze longingly through the window.

The white space was virtually empty, apart from the dark boxy silhouettes of a few men in suits. Waiters were dotted around with full trays of champagne, looking redundant and lost.

"Oh my God!" cried Deborah as they passed. "I could actually hear their footsteps!"

"It's seven o'clock, as well," Moira gasped. "It should be rammed by now."

"Well, this is what they wanted so badly," said Audrey self-righteously. "I hope they're really happy now with their fabulous empty shows. Just a few bankers. Wow, the art world's as funky as ever!"

Although they continued to grumble to each other as they bustled through the streets, something had been ignited inside all three women. Hope.

****

By October, the liggers had gradually been re-absorbed into the private view scene; the 'list' had been discreetly shelved and an unspoken symbiotic relationship had been established. The gallerists served canapés and drinks to rooms stuffed to the brim with joyful enthusiasts and the liggers generously forgave their former tormentors.

"I'm telling you, a bidet is for washing your arse in!" Thomas, the Swiss, declared one evening in the Sprooth McGowan gallery. He had just returned from a summer in France.

"No it isn't," challenged Audrey. "It's for your feet!"

"No, I'm telling you, all the French have really clean arses," Thomas argued, his bald head shone under the bright spot lighting.

"Well, I can vouch for that," Simon Baldwin chipped in.

There was a general movement away from the liggers by less outspoken guests, but this went unnoticed by the group itself, so entrenched were they in this cultural debate.

Baddie and Eustacia were outside, smoking Vogues with Grettil who had donned her trademark pilot's hat. Inside, Reverend George and Matthew of Mayfair were locked in conversation at the back of the gallery.

Matthew of Mayfair's colourful outfit was in stark contrast to the reverend's long black cassock. This communion of individualists was now an established part of Cork Street's fame and allure.

"Guys, it's so great that we're all together again," said Mac, putting his arms around Simon and Audrey, who stood within the central congregation.

"It certainly is," sighed Audrey blissfully. "We're back where we belong."

A bejeweled finger tapped Audrey on the shoulder; she jumped and turned, discovering a radiant Meryl.

Audrey screamed with delight, and each member of the group took it in turns to hug their long lost friend. She had remained abroad for months after the Biennale.

Thomas looked her up and down. "Did you win the lottery or something?"

Meryl smiled and did a twirl. Her hair was dyed blonde now and had been styled into relaxed curls; she wore a shimmering silver dress. As the liggers eyes travelled downwards, their screams of appreciation grew louder and louder. Meryl wore red, four-inch heeled sandals.

"I've been holidaying in Italy with this millionaire," she explained, bending over and tucking a stray bunion back under the straps. "He owns the entire estate of Frederico Beacon. He's loaded."

"So, you really did win the lottery then!" said Thomas.

"Well kind of, but you see, he turned out to be gay. He was Frederico's last lover, that's how he got all the inheritance," Meryl explained without a hint of discretion.

"So pass him over then," said Simon.

Meryl laughed. "Well, you can have him, but he's old enough to be your father and he lives in Florence. I was just there to make him appear as though he were straight throughout all the legal stuff, you know? I was the beard."

"Oh, sorry sweetheart," said Audrey, putting a hand on her arm.

"Oh, don't be sorry," said Meryl, sweeping her hand dismissively. "I got a new wardrobe, and rode on the back of his motorbike."

"Well, the culling's over!" boomed Mac cheerily, changing the subject.

"So, I see," said Meryl, with a deep nod. "Oh, and there's a very special event later this evening that you must all come to."

***

At eight thirty, the galleries closed their doors and all the liggers piled onto the number 340 bus. They were heading towards St Katherine's dock where, according to Meryl, a VIP event was underway.

Mac sat at the back of the bus with Grettil, Baddie and Eustacia. He was being savaged by Grettil – with whom he had established a precarious relationship - for enthusiastically suggesting that the four of them go to a museum one day.

"I'm an artist, not an American teenager," Grettil screamed at him, in response to his idea of a double date.

Baddie cackled, whilst Eustacia hiccupped.

"God, she's really bollocking him, isn't she?" said

Deborah disapprovingly from a few seats away.

"She's a bit insecure that lady," said Audrey. "Mac may soften her."

Eventually they alighted by the Thames and weaved through the backstreets towards St Katherine's.

A horn sounded as they entered the dock and their attention was caught by a most unusual sight.

An enormous black shiny vessel dominated the dancing waters. There were other big posh boats but this one towered above them, making them look like little toys. It was four or five stories high, each floor boasting a row of blacked out windows with a row of sparkling diamond lights beneath.

"What the fuck is that?" shrieked Eustacia.

"Batman's boat?" offered Baddie.

"Wow!" cried Mac "It's like a Jeff Koons."

To everyone's astonishment, Meryl went up to the front of this luxurious leviathan and waved her arms in the air. "Ahoy!" she whooped.

The pilot in the illuminated control room saluted and there was a loud whirring sound.

The black lacquer covering over the front deck gradually slid upwards and a grinning Peter Corbitt, attired in blazer and flannels, fists on hips, was revealed to the stunned assembly.

"Ta-daaa!" Meryl beamed. "Peter has finally returned to us after months in voluntary exile."

"How - what - blinking blimey!" stammered Ashpak.

"I went to Chioggia for this gala - as the beard - and bumped into none other than our friend here," explained Meryl as they made their way over to the yacht. "Peter had been in hiding for months after the Hurst series débacle at Charlie's thinking he was gunna get assassinated. Then, out of the blue, the chap who gave him the key to the boat in exchange for 'giving up the Hursts' - you know, Mr...?"

"Barbieri," gulped Mac.

"Yes, Mr Barbieri, and his entire ring were killed by a rival gang," finished Meryl triumphantly.

"Well, that was handy," said Deborah, raising a pair of poorly penciled eyebrows.

"Remember that funny masked stranger in the Giardini?" Meryl asked Ashpak. "Well, that was Peter, trying to talk to us, but he had to run off - that Violette Wu from Charlie's was behind us apparently."

"Well, speaking of which, we're basically all eternally blacklisted from Charlie's," said Mac remorsefully, his forehead creased.

"Oh come on, who needs Charlie's, when we've got Peter's yacht?"' sang Meryl joyfully, as a sparkly gangway was lowered hospitably in their direction. "Finally... our very own venue!"

Peter stepped out onto the top of the gangway, cutting a weedy silhouette against the bright lights from within. He raised a bottle of champagne into the air victoriously and looked on at the diverse troop of art and party lovers.

"Welcome aboard 'The Cork Street Wino'!"

The End

Also published by Thin Man Press

Peter Doherty's *From Albion to Shangri-La*
The Libertines and Babyshambles front man's private diaries and journals from 2008 – 2013.
Edited by Nina Antonia

This collection of uncensored words, accounts, thoughts and sub-conscious reflections from Doherty follows in the tradition of dangerous books by the likes of William Burroughs, Charles Bukowski, Alex Trocchi… all hailed now as great writers, yet back in the day their early titles courted an atmosphere of disapproval. The contents of Doherty's journals have much in common with these works: the ebb and flow of consciousness; the (often narcotic) dream states and confessional meanderings; the incisive analytical observation; the vivid sex scenes; the beautiful prose-poetry; and last, but not least the alarming misadventures of an artist in full confession. Doherty and his contemporaries (like Amy Winehouse and Peaches Geldof who are both free-styling contributors to the book) epitomised the nihilism of the noughties. *From Albion to Shangri-La* captures the filth and the fury as well as the poetry and the pathos.

"Drug-fuelled rantings." *Mail on Sunday*

Badshah Khan: Islamic Peace Warrior
by Heathcote Williams

A book-length 'investigative poem' about the amazing life and legacy of Badshah Abdel Gaffar Khan, Islamic Peace Warrior and friend of Mahatma Gandhi. As the violent excesses of Muslim extremist groups dominate the media, the best-selling author of *Whale Nation, Autogeddon, Royal Babylon et al* offers this timely account of another face Islam. Badshah Khan founded a 100,000 strong unarmed 'Peace Army' during India's 1940s sectarian conflict. This devout and prayerful Pashtun giant of a man's legacy as a spiritual guide and champion of world peace lives on in the hearts of millions of Muslims.

"Badshah Khan was a more remarkable leader than Mahatma Gandhi...Williams's easy to follow account outlines the story of this heroic figure about whom too little is known." *Independent*

"*Badshah Khan, Islamic Peace Warrior* deserves to be a best-seller... especially now." Professor Paul Rogers in *Open Democracy.*

The One & Only: Peter Perrett, Homme Fatale
by Nina Antonia
With a new introduction by John Cooper-Clarke

This revised, expanded and updated edition of Nina Antonia's 1996 cult classic is a roller-coaster ride through one of rock's wildest, most unpredictable careers. Antonia also explores the personal relationships behind the headlines, in particular Peter and Xena Perrett's amazingly enduring 45 year marriage. Granted full access to the reclusive Only Ones front man and everyone who matters in his story, Antonia unflinchingly traces his path from privileged childhood to drug dealer; from musical obscurity to decadent rock icon submerged in narcotic slumbers in an antique-filled mansion… before the dream spectacularly fell apart.

"A richly detailed account that effortlessly negotiates Perrett's private peccadilloes and his public life." *Mojo*

"Riveting stuff..." *Record Collector*

A Wave of Dreams
by Louis Aragon

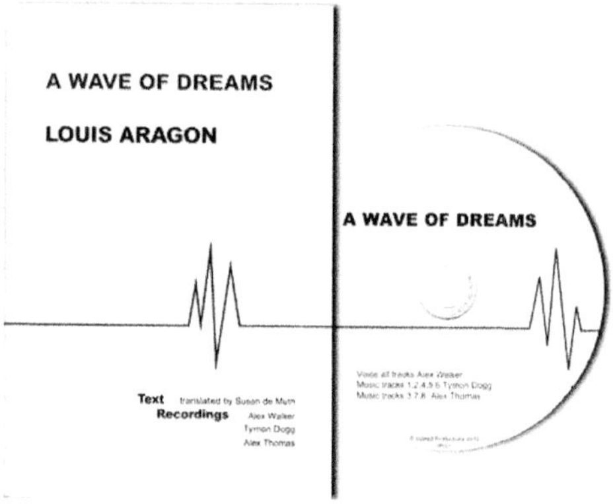

Louis Aragon's 1924 prose-poem-essay (*Une vague de rêves*) is a compelling, lyrical, first-hand account of the early days of surrealist experimentation in Paris. Aragon vividly describes, and philosophically evaluates, the inner adventures, the hallucinations and encounters with 'the Marvellous' which took the young surrealists to the brink of insanity as a revolutionary new era in Art History was born. This beautifully presented little art-house book contains a complimentary CD of eight extracts from the test, spoken by actor Alex Walker and evocatively set in musical soundscapes by Tymon Dogg and Alex Thomas.

"A leftfield treat…mysteriously opaque and strangely lovely." Thomas H Green, *Daily Telegraph.*

Spark in the Dark
by John Constable

Best known for his *Southwark Mysteries*, playwright John Constable is also an accomplished poet, satirist, and writer of colourful dramatic prose.

Spark In The Dark is his first collection of poems and prose poems, including *Wennefer, a* hallucinatory, visceral, cautionary tale, retelling the Isis and Osiris myth in contemporary south London club culture.

"Like Shakespeare on acid." *Time Out*

"Past and present, sacred and profane jostle and collide in a glorious tumult… couched in verse that is muscular, ribald, and often dazzlingly rich…" *The Times*

The Rise & Fall of The Clash
by Danny Garcia

In 1983 at the height of their fame and success the Clash disintegrated.

This book tells the story of what happened…

Spanish film maker Danny Garcia ('The Legend of Johnny Thunders', 'Six Bullets to Hell') gained exclusive interviews with – among other - Mick Jones (with whom Garcia spent several weeks); legendary manager Bernie Rhodes and Pearl Harbor, Paul Simenon's girlfriend at the time, whose analysis of what went on between Mick and Joe Strummer and then Joe and the rest of the band is razor sharp, and delivered with eloquence and humor.

The book also contains previously unseen photos of The Clash both before and after Mick Jones got sacked.

"Featuring the heights of tragedy and comedy worthy of a Shakesperean drama." *Chris Salewicz, author, broadcaster, journalist and official Joe Strummer biographer.*

Licentia

by A.A. Walker

An exquisitely evocative, erotic, hallucinogenic, dramatic prose-poem that embroils the reader in a kaleidoscope of intersecting relationships and events. Baroque characters in a variety of guises people a dream that tugs at the heart strings with surrealist abandon, grace, excitement and wonder.

'Imagination unbound, Licentia is the enemy of conformity. Read and be free. As intoxicating as a thousand years of incense and poppies; A. A. Walker has fulfilled the poet's eternal calling.'

Nina Antonia, music writer, author.

Guarding bin Laden: My Life in al-Qaeda

by Nasser al-Bahri, bin Laden's former bodyguard

Nasser al-Bahri spent four years in the heart of al-Qaeda, most of them at Osama bin Laden's side. In *Guarding bin Laden: My Life in al-Qaeda*, Bahri gives a dramatic account of daily life in the terror group's secret HQ and training camps. He details al-Qaeda's organizational structure, extraordinary security measures and their arrangements with the Pakistani Army and security services.

Yet this is a personal story too…Bahri reveals how he gradually became disenchanted with violent extremism, falling out with bin Laden and eventually leaving the organization shortly before 9/11, hoping to take his wife and new baby to live a 'normal' life back home in Yemen. Instead, he was arrested on arrival in Sana'a.

"An extraordinary first-hand account of life at the heart of the terrorist organisation," *Le Figaro Magazine*

All books available from Amazon, bookshops or direct from the publisher

www.thinmanpress.com

info@thinmanpress.com

Printed in Great Britain
by Amazon

21839751R00067